The First Hurt

The First Hurt

Stories by Rachel Sherman

OPEN CITY BOOKS

New York

Printed in the United States of America

These stories were previously published as follows: "The Reaper" in *n+1*; "Two Stories; Single Family; Scenic View" and "Keeping Time" in *Open City*; "Homestay" in *Post Road*; "Proof" in *Small Spiral Notebook*; "The Neutered Bulldog" in *McSweeney's*.

Design by Nick Stone
Cover photograph: *Providence, Rhode Island*, 1975–1978,
by Francesca Woodman. Courtesy of Betty and George Woodman.
Author photograph by Laura Rose

Library of Congress Cataloging-in-Publication Data
Sherman, Rachel, 1975–
   The first hurt : stories / by Rachel Sherman.
      p. cm.
   ISBN-10: 1-890447-41-2 (pbk.)
   ISBN-13: 978-1-890447-41-0 (pbk.)
   I. Title.
   PS3619.H466F57 2006
   813'.6—dc22   2006002585

OPEN CITY BOOKS
270 Lafayette Street
New York, NY 10012
www.opencity.org

First Edition
06 07 08 09 10   10 9 8 7 6 5 4 3 2 1

Open City Books are published by Open City, Inc., a nonprofit corporation, and are distributed to the trade by Publishers Group West. This book was published with support from the Literary Ventures Fund.

For my parents

TABLE OF CONTENTS

The Reaper

Sergeant Daniel Burkhart's letters fly over two oceans and two states in a plane. They fly in cargo and wait in trucks. When they finally make it they sit in the mailbox at the end of Beth's driveway. Cars drive by.

On days Beth gets home before her mother they are safe. They are still white, still whole and unopened. Sometimes there is only one. On good days: two.

On days when her mother is not home she runs inside and hides the letters in the drawers that are built inside her platform bed. The bed matches the walls and the walls match the curtains. Everything is mauve except for the carpet, which has a big white spot on it from nail-polish remover she once spilled.

Her mother waits for her to get home. She sits on the couch the way she did when she found the diet pills.

"Beth," she says. "You got three letters today."

Her mother holds them out to her. They are not opened.

"I want to know what's going on," her mother says. "Is he writing to you *dirty?*"

Beth does not answer. She walks up the stairs and locks her bedroom door.

She lies on her stained carpet and lines up her letters on the floor.

They do not reek of the heat that Daniel Burkhart has written in. All three smell of the cold fall air.

Beth has wine stains shaped like two islands: birthmarks on her face. One circles her eyeball. The other one is a red dot, spotted on her cheek like the makeup of a clown.

The birthmarks have lightened since she was born. They still turn purple in warm water.

When she is home alone she takes blue and gold and purple eye shadow and colors her birthmarks in. She looks for countries on maps that might be shaped like them. She searches spills, clouds, and leaves.

There had been talk of burning. Doctors had mentioned using a laser across her face. But then there was fear of hurting her eye.

She would rather see. Read the letter. Let the kids call her Creeper. In her mother's bathroom, she looks at herself on the side of her face that is clear. She puts another mirror on the other side of her face. Her profile goes on and on, clean and pretty. The other way shows a million girls all looking at the girl with the spots on her face next to her.

When the war started, her father put a clear sticker on his back window.

"I Support the Troops!" it said.

Her mother did not support them and drove the other car.

When the letters come up on a frozen-dinner night her father supports her mother.

"So what's this Mom's been telling me?" he asks.

"I'm doing an assignment for school," Beth says, looking down at the low-cal sauce drying up into what looks like a red scar on the chicken skin.

It is true. Beth is writing to a soldier so she can get extra credit for a psych class she is trying to avoid failing in advance.

"What kind of assignment?" her father asks.

Her mother looks at her with hard eyes and pursed lips and a blonde moustache that she bleaches every Friday.

"For psychology. We get extra credit to write letters to a soldier," she tells him.

"Tell him how many letters," her mother says, looking at her father, then at her.

Beth tells her father that she has written a few, and that he has sent a few back.

"A few? Elliott, she gets two to three letters every day!"

Her father, with his hands on the table, with his close-cropped nails, with his gray hair, looks at his daughter.

"What is he saying to you, Elizabeth?" he asks.

Dear Beth,

Thanks for your letters. Keep 'em coming! I can't tell you how boring it is over here.

Yes, of course I miss my wife. My kid, too. But it is much more interesting to hear about you.

It sounds like you had a nice time bowling with Sandra the other night. Be careful of those boys! They're animals!

I wanted to tell THIS IS THE REAPER!!!! I HAVE TAKEN OVER DAN'S BODY!!!! HE HAS NO CONTROL OVER ME. WILL YOU SEND ME A PAIR OF YOUR PANTIES?

The First Hurt

Oh, my goodness!!! I can't believe what just happened. I am so so so so sorry. Sometimes I am taken over by another entity. His name is the Reaper, and he is a dirty fellow. I apologize—I am not accountable. Please forgive me. I will try not to let him out again.

Beth put the letter down and touched her face. How could he have known? It was as if Daniel Burkhart had flown, sandy and tan, across two oceans and land, past the dump and the beach and the fields, to her school. There, brushing the sand from his army pants and shoes, he had walked into her psych class where the teacher called her name. It was as if she had looked up, and the teacher called on her.

"Creeper," the boy next to her whispered.

It is as if Sergeant Daniel heard him.

It is like he flew back across the oceans with his hands out like Superman. He saw the earth small and blue and green, then landed back on the base. He fell onto his army-clothed bottom bunk and lay down with his hand behind his head. Sand in his fingernails as if he had never left, he sat up to write to her.

He thought about "Creeper." It would be too mean.

"Reaper," he thought. It was close.

Dear Beth—

I liked your last letter. You are funny. Really.

I'll tell you, mostly there is just a lot of sitting around here doing nothing. I play cards and THIS IS THE REAPER! WHEN I AM BORED I MASTURBATE AND THINK ABOUT YOU. BELOW IS A LIST OF QUESTIONS. YOU MUST ANSWER THEM ALL.

I'm so sorry. Oh my God. I can't believe that just happened again. Please forgive me. I am trying hard to control him.

Here are some questions I've been meaning to ask. I hope you can still trust me.

1–What is your favorite food?

2–What is your favorite song?

3–What is your favorite fruit?

4–REAPER QUESTION: DO YOU MASTURBATE IN THE BATH OR THE SHOWER?

5–What is your favorite color?

6–What is your favorite subject in school?

7–What is your favorite rock group?

8–REAPER QUESTION: CAN YOU LICK YOUR OWN PUSSY?

9–If you could live anywhere, where would it be?

In psychology class the teacher videotapes each student walking across the room so he can talk about what their body language says to the world.

"Who is going to be first?" the teacher says. He has skinny legs and wears cowboy boots.

Beth can feel her palms sweat. Then she sees that the camera is set up so that it will only show her good side.

Sandra goes first. Sandra is older and boys like her. She started school midyear after leaving Holy Name. She is wearing white pants that have brown and green stains on the butt from sitting on the grass and on the steps.

"Shake that ass," one boy says, and even the teacher laughs.

Sandra walks in a way that Beth has memorized but cannot imitate. She heard that Sandra had a hole in her nose from doing too much coke.

When it is Beth's turn everyone gets quiet. She walks and smiles, as if she has two good sides on one face.

When everyone is done walking they sit and watch themselves walk on the screen.

They watch Sandra.

"See how she is?" the teacher says. "She is confident."

When they play Beth back on the screen she waits for someone to say something.

"Now see how Beth's head is turned down?" the teacher says, pointing to her head that is as big as his finger on the TV screen.

There are a few good seconds where you cannot see the mark.

"You look good!" Sandra says.

"See how Beth moves? You can tell from her posture she is shy," the teacher says.

"Creeper," a boy says.

Sandra leans over and whispers to Beth, "You just need makeup."

Before the bell the teacher claps his hands.

"Has anyone heard from their soldiers?" he asks.

Sergeant Burkhart asks her for a picture.

The Reaper says: *SEND ME A PICTURE OF YOUR NAKED TITS!!!*

She is polite to the Sergeant, putting on her mother's pancake makeup so that you can hardly see where her birthmark is. She puts her mother's silky green shirt on, then balances the camera between her knees while she lies on her parents' bed.

The camera snaps her up and spits her behind the black curtain of the Polaroid.

There she appears: clean and blurry and ready to fly.

1—Pizza or chicken, I guess.
2—I don't have one favorite.

3–Grapefruit.

4–

5–Purple

Beth walks home and opens the back door where the house air bites her face.

"Beth?" she hears her mother. It is her angry voice.

Beth runs up to her room. She goes into the drawers beneath her bed and checks under the note that she had written in case her mom tried to snoop:

STAY AWAY YOU FUCKING DIRTY BITCH I DON'T GO THROUGH YOUR THINGS!!!!!

But the letters are there.

Dear Beth,

I loved your picture. Thank you so much for sending it.

I'm sorry I can't send you one. We can't take pictures here. Tell me more about school THIS IS THE REAPER! IT IS NOT DAN'S FAULT THAT I KEEP COMING OUT. WHAT HAPPENED TO THE NAKED PICTURE?

Sorry, sorry, sorry. I am so sorry, Beth.

"We need to talk to you," Beth's mother yells, knocking on the door.

When Beth does not answer, her mother gets louder.

"Unlock the door!" she yells. She tries to turn the knob.

Beth turns off the lights and lies down on her bed. Above her is the stucco ceiling, the roof, and then the sky. Across two oceans, a war is going on. It isn't an exciting war like the one her parents watched. This war seems as unreal as the photo of her mother wearing a white flower halo when she was supposedly marching for peace.

The First Hurt

Dear Sergeant Daniel Burkhart,
I really think you should write more to your wife. Does she know about the Reaper?

When Beth's mother has yelled her last yell of the night, Beth closes her eyes. She floats through nighttime into daytime, all the way to the sky above the Bermuda Triangle.

"Were you worried?" Daniel Burkhart asks as they fly holding each other's hands like parachuters do on their way down.

They don't have to scream in the Bermuda Triangle.

"No," she lies.

They are falling but not falling. The earth does not get any closer.

He could have been ugly.

"I'm happy you are here," she says.

When they land, suddenly, in the desert somewhere, he traces the outline of her face and points to the sky. There, it is night. The stars make her shape.

6–English
7–Probably the Beastie Boys. Also, Led Zeppelin.
8–
9–Florida or Italy

"What does everyone think about the war?" Beth's psychology teacher asks. He walks between the desks in his cowboy boots and jeans.

"It sucks!" a boy says.

"Yeah, my soldier says he hates it there," Sandra says. She reaches into her pocketbook that is big and sounds like it is full of coins and keys.

"What else do your soldiers say?" he asks.

Sandra leans over and whispers-laughs to Beth, "That he's horny."

"Girls?" the teacher says, looking at Beth and Sandra, "Do you have something to say?"

"Our soldiers are looooonely," Sandra whines.

After class, Sandra taps Beth's shoulder. "C'mon," she says, "I need a cigarette."

Beth follows her outside, ducking under the school windows and then waiting until the social studies teacher looks away to dash into the woods.

They run and the things inside Sandra's bag bang loudly against each other. When they get to where no one can see, Sandra lights a cigarette and gives it to Beth.

"You like menthols?" she asks, lighting her own cigarette.

Beth nods and takes a drag.

They sit on a log that all the kids sit on in the woods, and Sandra reaches into her big bag and takes out a picture from inside her wallet.

"Check this out," she says, handing it to Beth.

The photo is of a man in army fatigues with his penis hanging out of his zipper and his arms above his head, pointing.

"That's my soldier. His name is Tom." Sandra points with her fake nail.

"He sent you this?" Beth asks. "They let him take pictures?"

Sandra laughs. "Of course he can take pictures. It's not top secret."

She takes the picture from Beth and looks at it.

Beth wonders where her picture is. It is supposed to be taped beneath the bottom of the top bunk of Sergeant Burkhart's tightly tucked bed. At night he is supposed to look up at it and wonder where it was that she had taken it. He is supposed to shine his flashlight on it to see her in a circle and bright in the dark.

"Isn't he huge?" Sandra asks, holding the photo out and putting her nail right below his waist.

Beth wonders where his picture is. It is supposed to be licked inside one of his envelopes, between two sheets of paper for protection. It is supposed to be hidden beneath her bed in a drawer and taken out when she was safe inside her locked room. It is supposed to show him smiling at her with his short hair and army gear, sitting on a fence like on a ranch with the desert endless behind him.

"I think I may join the army after I graduate," Sandra says. "Tom says he may be able to pull some strings so that I can be in his squad. You get total benefits AND free medical."

In the mailbox are bills and magazines and a letter. As always, it is addressed in black, block letters to Beth.

Her mother's car is not in the driveway, so she runs into the house, up the stairs to her room. After locking her door, she lies on the nail-polish stain on her carpet and puts the letter in front of her.

One today. Licked with Daniel's tongue.

Beth holds the letter to her nose and thinks about Sandra and her soldier. She wonders if every girl has a matching soldier. She wonders if over there, in sand and tents, there are men just waiting to pick up the letter that will lead to their other half, the girl they have been waiting for, living a life that fits their own on the other side of the world.

The soldier she has found is split inside himself. He has found her.

Dear Beth,

How are you? I'm bored. It is very hot here and we have a bug problem. And no, the food is pretty gross, but we don't have to eat out of cans. We have a cook that makes a lot of spaghetti.

We don't get to do too many sports here, although I have been really into Ping-Pong lately.

More questions:

1—What is your astrological sign?

2—Do you have a pet?

On Friday afternoon, she hears her mother read his words: "DO YOU HAVE A VIBRATOR?"

Her mother speaks quietly, in a whine.

In Beth's room, her box beneath her bed is empty. In the kitchen, her mother reads to her father.

"Oh, and here is a nice one: 'Do you have a favorite brand of car?'"

Beth watches her parents from a crack in the kitchen door.

She watches her parents hold her letters in their hands.

"What do we do with the letters?" her mother asks.

Her father takes one, then another, and crumples them into balls.

"I don't want them here," he says, walking to the sink and turning on the water. He puts them in so they turn wet and pulpy. Capital and lowercase letters smear into blue water-colors. Beth watches as he takes them out, hanging down like thick fabric, and puts them in the trash basket.

Tomorrow the garbage men will take them, still damp, drying, hardening again, out past the mailbox, past the high school, to the dump. The paper will be ground by then, mixed with dirt and diapers and bad meat.

The First Hurt

Beth walks upstairs and lies on her carpet. She reaches out to cover the stain from the nail-polish remover. Without the stain, the floor is a sea of mauve. She remembers when they first got the carpet, a long time ago. She lay on her bed and leaned off to rub the fibers back and forth, making it dark then light.

A long time ago, when she was born, the doctor held her and slapped her face to start her breathing. When her cheek faded from his red, hard hand, there she was with her marks, crying for her mother.

Just recently, a man in the desert felt the crumple of his heart far away. He felt the sting of disappointment when his mailbox was empty. He felt the sand around him shake with war, and his bunk collapse while he slept.

Sergeant Burkhart found himself above the Bermuda Triangle. He found himself lost in a tornado of women who flew and men who were lost. He found himself spinning until he was alone, and then he heard the sound of his own voice.

Beth hums and listens to herself. Whoever will love her will love listening to her sing, she thinks. He will love twisting her hair into curls. He will be someone who will talk to her about the old stone house they will spend summers in someday, and sometimes they will meet in their dreams just to hold each other's hands.

Two Stories; Single Family; Scenic View

My wife, Beth, knew something was wrong, she told me, but she ignored it. She drove home from her job where she was a plastic-surgery nurse and went to sleep. She ignored it, she said, when it felt like a bubble bursting, then like she had to pee, then throw up, then die.

This was all after the fact, after they had had to remove the babies early and take them away before we could even hold them.

There was something wrong with both of our twins. The boy we named Jonathan seemed slow. The girl's feet turned in awkwardly and the doctor said she might never learn to walk. They came out so small at first, they thought the babies might die.

My job was an hour away, an hour and a half at rush hour. I drove on the freeway, listening to talk radio. I woke early so I could go to the gym first, then off to the office where I was in charge of sales for a large air conditioning company. I had a secretary who was a grandma type. I had a picture of Beth from when we were first married on my desk.

When the twins first came home, we put them in a room that my wife decorated: a pink side for the girl, a blue one for the boy. When they cried after we put them to bed, my wife ignored them. She was training them, she said, to sleep at night, so I ignored them too. I liked them, and sometimes I wanted to hold them. Sometimes I wanted to get between them, one baby beneath each of my arms, and lie down in our bed, but my wife said they couldn't sleep with us because we might crush them.

Three weeks after we brought them home, Beth brought the babies to the doctor again. That night she told me how it was her fault things went wrong. Then she told me what the doctor said: that Jonathan had lost air when blood had flooded into his part of her belly. She said that they didn't want to give a name to the problems Emily had. Yet.

We were on the deck, sipping white wine. We had a pool and lived in southern California in a new development that looked out over a big piece of dirt land. One day our view would be crowded with houses just like ours.

Our house was on the first set of streets that were built. The houses were the same inside, but my wife had decorated ours in her own way. When friends came over, they were impressed by how she had the time to do it all: work, mother, and even decorate. I looked out onto the land. There were still shrubs growing there. They hadn't finished building the pool, but it would be done soon.

We had bought the house right before the babies were born so Beth could get it ready. The other houses on the street were just starting to fill up. When I walked the twins in their carriage on weekends, I waved to our new neighbors and sometimes stopped to talk. You couldn't tell there was something wrong with the twins yet, so all the women cooed over them, asked to hold them, kissed the top of their downy heads. Sometimes I took them past our development and over to the hill where new developments were being built.

I was careful to hold their stroller tight. I would lock the wheels, then sit down next to them and point to the sky and the clouds. I would say the words "sky" and "cloud" and make funny faces to make them smile.

While my wife took her weekend naps, I told my children stories about how tiny they had been at first, how they had been strapped with tubes in the nursery for weeks because their mother, who was supposed to be on bed rest, had decided to work instead.

It was hard to be mad at my wife. She was busy, and cheerful, and seemed to have an answer for everything that had to do with the twins. She had tried to breastfeed at first, lying on the carpet in the living room and pumping her breast pump. She had breast implants a few years before that her boss had given her for free since it was good advertising for the patients. She also had her lips tattooed in pink so that when she woke in the morning, she looked like she had already put makeup on.

The breast pump didn't work, so we fed the babies formula. On weekends and at night we would each take a baby in our laps and let them suck, hungrily, happily, on their bottles. They would drool and slurp, trying to get bigger and better. They had certain feeding times, but sometimes I wondered if we should feed them more.

One Saturday, while walking the twins down the street, I saw a moving truck outside a new home.

"Hey," I waved to a man with no shirt on who was coming out of the house.

The man had a brown mustache and a hairy chest. We shook hands; we both had sturdy grips.

"I'm Hal," he said.

"Welcome to the neighborhood, Hal," I said, "I'm Mike. We live down at number eight."

Hal looked down at the twins and smiled. "Looks like you got yourself a handful," he said.

Then Emily started to cry so I undid the belt and picked her up while Jonathan slept.

"Mary!" Hal turned around to his house and said, "Come meet our new neighbors!"

A woman came out from the house with black hair tied up in a ponytail. She was overweight, but with a pretty face.

She shook my hand with light, cool fingers, and I saw that she had strange green eyes.

"Oh, look at these gorgeous babies!" she said, taking Emily from my arms and rocking her until she stopped crying.

"God, I need a break," Hal said. "Want a beer?"

I pushed the double stroller with Jonathan still sleeping in it up the driveway and into their backyard. Their pool was finished and had a waterfall made of fake rocks. We sat on the grass and Mary brought out a cooler. I put Emily on her stomach so she could roll around.

"My wife decorated our place," I told them. "She's done a great job. You'll have to come over for a barbecue."

Hal and Mary told me how they worked at a grocery store but had saved up for years to buy a house.

I told them about my job in sales and about my wife and her job as a plastic-surgery nurse.

"Wow!" Mary said. "She must have some interesting stories."

Before the babies, my wife and I would go out to dinner on the weekends. We would drink wine and she would tell me funny stories about her job. Once she told me that a man had come into her office and wanted breast implants on his back. I liked to look at my wife across the table, laughing while she talked. This seemed like such a long time ago.

Suddenly, Jonathan woke up and began to cry. Loud music came from the front of the house.

Mary said, "Oh, I'm so sorry. That's our daughter and her boyfriend."

Car doors slammed, and a girl giggled. Mary rolled her eyes.

"Kelly! Come back around. Meet our new neighbors," Hal said.

I looked behind me as a girl opened the gate on the side of the house. She wore only the top part of a bikini with shorts and her bellybutton was pierced. A black guy with no shirt and a carved-out body followed behind her.

"Hey," the girl said, kneeling down next to us. Her breasts were the kind that held themselves up. Natural.

She picked up Emily and bounced her up and down.

"They are gorgeous!" she said.

Introductions went all around.

I shook the black guy's hand.

"Elvis," he said with a strong, dry palm. He nodded his head.

"I'll get us some beers," Kelly said. She got up and walked inside. Her ass was huge and came out of her like fake breasts on her behind.

After a few beers, I told them how I needed to wake my wife, so I put the twins back in their carriage and strapped them into their seats. Then I walked out to the front of their house where Kelly's black sports car was parked.

The top of the car was down so I looked inside. There were menthol cigarettes on the armrest. The license plate said "MCBOOTY."

When I got home I put the babies in their cribs. They cried so I closed their door. I went into our bedroom, which Beth had decorated in a leopard, safari-like theme. She had put candles in tall dark wood holders, but we hadn't gotten a chance to light them yet.

Beth had not wanted to have sex since she had the babies. She wore big pajamas to bed and turned away when I tried to touch her. When she was asleep I jerked off next to her, my thigh touching her on her thigh, and concentrated on that one small part of me I could feel her with.

In the bedroom Beth was lying down in her sweatshirt and watching TV.

"Hey," I said, taking off my clothes and climbing into the bed next to her.

"Where were you?" she asked, not looking at me.

"Oh, I met some new neighbors. You would like them. Nice, down-to-earth people. Hal and Mary," I started to rub her arm but she pulled it away.

"Great," she said. "You smell like beer. You could have called me."

"I'm sorry," I said. "I thought I'd let you sleep."

"Whatever," she said, getting out of the bed. "I'm going to order fish tacos and pick them up. What do you want?"

I went in to look at the twins while Beth went out, but they had already fallen asleep. When she came home we went out to the deck and ate our dinner. We drank wine, watched TV, and went to bed.

The next day was Sunday. I took the kids out again for our walk. Instead of going out of the development, I walked to Hal and Mary's house and rang the doorbell. Kelly's car was in the driveway.

"Hey, neighbor," Hal said when he opened the door.

He was shirtless again and motioned me inside. I parked the carriage on the lawn and unstrapped the babies. Hal picked up Jonathan and I picked up Emily.

"Want a beer?" he asked as I followed him inside.

"Sure," I said.

Their house was the same as ours except on the opposite side of the street. This meant that it was also turned around: a mirror reflection of our place.

They had done a lot of unpacking in only a few days. They had had the front hall painted a pinkish color. Mary was arranging dolls on the mantle piece.

Mary took one of the dolls and brought it up to Emily. She made the doll's hands wave, "Hello! How are you?"

I followed Hal into the kitchen.

"Mary does the decorating," Hal said, winking and giving me a beer.

The kitchen had stools by the counter, and white wallpaper with small blue whales on it. In our development you pick from a selection of different paints and wallpaper. The builders put it up for you before you even move in. Beth had picked tan for our living room; Mary had picked dark green.

"This was my idea," he said, pointing to a big fish above the TV. "I caught this one—had it stuffed."

We walked out to the backyard where they had already set up their lawn furniture. Kelly and Elvis were swimming in the pool.

Hal talked about fishing and I watched as Elvis threw Kelly up in the water. I watched as she got out and then dove off the side of the pool.

When they got out of the water, Kelly put a towel around her waist and twisted her hair around and around like a towel to get the water out. Hal handed both Kelly and Elvis a beer.

Kelly took Emily and bounced her on her knees.

"You're so lucky to have twins!" she said.

I wondered when what was wrong with the babies would begin to show. They still couldn't crawl.

I told them how the twins had been premature and in the hospital for a long time before we could bring them home. Kelly listened and nodded, and Elvis took Jonathan and held him up in the air.

"I would love to have twins," Kelly said, rubbing Elvis's knee. "We're engaged, but we haven't gotten the ring yet."

"Congratulations," I said, watching as they held my babies.

The gate on the side of the house made a loud sound and we all turned toward it. Beth, wearing a bikini top and a sarong, walked into the backyard.

"Hi," she waved. "I'm the wife."

She came over and kissed me on the mouth. I could smell wine on her breath. Then she took Emily from Kelly's arms, smiling with her lips closed.

I introduced everyone to Beth and she waved.

"Have a seat," Elvis said, getting up for her to sit down.

"Thank you," she said. Once she had told me she liked Shaquille O'Neal, which surprised me. I watched Beth's eyes to see if she was looking at Elvis. I looked at Kelly and caught Beth's eyes on mine.

Mary came out and we drank some more. She put chips on the table and Kelly put a bunch in her hand and ate them all. Beth sipped her wine.

We talked about the development and how the realtor had promised that in a few years more businesses would move out here. When the development was finished, there might even be a mall.

It was getting dark, and the babies began to cry. I told our new neighbors that we would love to have them over some time.

As we were leaving, I watched Kelly and Elvis jump back in the pool. I saw Elvis pick Kelly up again, the pool lights on her. She put her feet and hands out like a statue or an ice skater. She became completely still, her face looking up at the sky. He held her in the air in his hands like that for only a moment, then grabbed her waist and threw her back in.

After we put the kids to bed, Beth broke out another bottle of wine.

"Boy, babe," I said, "I'm tired."

"Fine!" she said, pouring herself a glass. Her sarong had fallen off and she stood in the kitchen in her red bikini. Her Caesarian scar had faded, but I could still see it. It reminded me of how stubborn she was when the doctor had told her to stop moving.

My wife had a bruise on her thigh.

"What?!" she asked, standing there.

"Nothing," I said.

I wished our pool was ready. I had called the contractors twice on Friday. I would call them again tomorrow.

Beth sat down in the den and turned on the TV.

"You know," she said above the sound, "that Kelly is a little whore. Did you see her license plate?"

"McBooty," I said.

"She has the biggest ass I've ever seen. Someone should put her on a diet."

My wife's body was thin and curved but she was not shaped like Kelly.

"McBooty!" my wife snorted and laughed. "What the fuck is that?"

The next night I got home from work early and took the kids out while Beth made dinner.

"Don't be long," she said. She was in a good mood and making pork tenderloin. She had dressed up and painted her fingernails.

I walked the kids down to Hal and Mary's. Kelly was in the driveway wearing the same jean shorts and bikini top she was wearing the night before. She was watering the plants with the hose.

"Hey," she said.

She came over to look at the kids.

"What does your license plate mean?" I asked. Elvis was not around.

"Oh," she said, standing up, "the kids used to call me that in high school, you know, cause my ass . . . "

"Oh," I said, "so the name stuck?"

"I guess," she said, laughing.

"I'm just taking the kids for a walk before dinner. Beth is making pork loin," I said.

"That's nice," she said.

"I better get back," I said, and started the stroller up the hill. Then I felt water on my back. I turned around and Kelly was standing with her legs spread, holding the hose like a gun, laughing with the setting sun behind her.

"What happened to your shirt?" Beth asked. She picked the twins up one at a time and put them in their high chairs.

"Oh, Kelly spritzed me while I was walking the twins."

"That big ass girl needs some serious lipo," she said.

Jonathan squirmed, trying to use his arms.

"Hands down!" she yelled, suddenly, hitting Jonathan on his arms. "Down!"

Jonathan began to cry and Beth took two bowls of Spaghettio's out of the microwave. She put one bowl on each of their trays.

Beth had set up the dining room with candles. She turned the stereo on to classical music and left the kitchen.

"We'll eat in here," she said.

"We won't be able to hear the kids," I said, following her into the dining room.

"Oh, they're fine," she said.

We had a babysitter from Tuesdays through Thursdays. Monday and Friday, Beth stayed home from work to watch the kids. Their nanny was sweet and made them homemade soups. I would eat their leftovers sometimes when I got home.

Beth brought out the tenderloin and salad, and we drank red wine and ate. Later, for a surprise, she brought out a chocolate cake.

Drinking, I noticed the grains in the table, my fingers, the way Beth looked in the glow of the candles. I could separate the colors on her face into different zones, like states on a map.

Beth smiled when I looked at her.

"What?" she asked, gently.

"Nothing," I said, and I could tell she thought I was thinking something nice.

When everything was done, I followed her into the kitchen. The babies were still in their high chairs, both leaning out of them, sideways, asleep. They had Spaghettio's all over their hands and faces.

"I'll just dunk them in the bath," my wife said.

"Isn't it too late?" I asked.

She ignored me and picked Emily out of her chair. I followed, holding Jonathan. She lay Emily down on the bathroom rug and stripped her. Emily woke up, crying, while Beth put her inside the bathtub and started the water. It was nine o'clock already. We usually put the kids down by seven.

"Give me him," she said and did the same to Jonathan. She took a sponge and began to scrub their faces. The twins did not seem to be looking anywhere. Their eyes were wet and wouldn't look at me.

When Beth was done we wrapped them up, all wet and tired, into towels. The top of Emily's head was soft and smelled like soap.

We dressed them in footsy pajamas and put them in their cribs.

"I'm beat," I said.

I got into bed and Beth came out of the bathroom dressed in a purple see-through gown. With the bathroom light still on behind her I could see everything.

"Wow!" I said.

She came over to me and I lifted her onto me and began to lick her.

I could hear her making the sounds she used to make, and I brought her down to kiss me.

"Ouch," she said, suddenly. "Your stubble hurts. Don't you ever fucking shave anymore?"

She turned over, and when I tried to hold her she pushed me away.

"What's wrong?" I asked.

"Nothing," she said.

"Are you angry?" I asked.

"You know why," she said, quietly.

We had two twins with real problems and it was all her fault. We lived in a nice neighborhood so there was no reason for her to get mad at that. I bought her the things she asked for and I liked the way she decorated the house. She hit my kids who had something wrong with them and they cried, but I didn't get angry. My babies cried, unable to control where their hands went, which made their mother mad.

"I don't know why, Beth," I said.

"Well, then, if you don't know, there is nothing I can do about it."

I lay there, listening to her whimper. I began to touch myself on my side of the bed. She cried and cried and I took myself down the street where I picked Kelly up in her pool and held her above me, light as a dove.

The next morning, I woke at my usual time and went to the gym. I watched myself in the mirror. I went to the office and had a usual day. I drove home to my wife and two children.

When I went in the house I found Beth at the kitchen table, crying.

"They know!" she yelled.

"What?" I asked. "Know what?" I went over to Beth who let me hold her while she sobbed into my shoulder.

I waited for her to catch her breath, running my hands down on her spine. She felt small and fragile and good.

"The . . . the kids. Someone said something today . . . I saw two ladies talking in the grocery store . . . they could tell there was something wrong with Jonathan."

"What about Emily?" I asked.

"What the fuck does that matter?" she yelled, looking at me with black eye makeup running down her cheek. Her next procedure was supposed to be tattooed-on eye shadow.

She ran into the bedroom and I followed her. The door to the twins' room was open but they weren't in their cribs.

"Where are the twins?" I asked.

Beth was on the bed with her head in her hands.

"I left them with your new friends," she said. "I needed to be alone."

"You mean Hal and Mary?" I said. "They're babysitting?"

"Yes!" she yelled.

I was confused, but I did not want her to get angrier.

I walked over to the bed and sat down next to her and began to rub her back.

"They're our babies," I said, "and we love them. It doesn't matter what other people think."

Beth looked up at me again from the leopard bedspread.

"Are you a fucking idiot!?" she yelled.

I stopped rubbing her back and put my hands in my lap. There was no reason for her to be angry at me.

I got up from the bed and walked out of the house to get Emily and Jonathan. I did not want to impose on Mary and Hal. I tried to imagine our babies the way a stranger would see them. I wondered if you could really tell that something was wrong.

Kelly was sitting on the front lawn, smoking a menthol cigarette.

"Hey," she yelled, waving at me. She was wearing a different bathing suit top but the same jean shorts.

"Jonathan and Emily are sleeping inside," she said.

"Good," I said. They were safe.

I sat down on the grass next to Kelly. The ground felt nice and I felt tired. I looked over at Kelly who stubbed the cigarette in the ground. She smiled at me but didn't say anything.

I began to tell her that I had a dream where at first, it seemed to be taking place at my house, but then everything turned around, and it was at hers. I told her how we were swimming in the dream, she and I, in the pool. In my dream, the waterfall was bigger than it really was and there was a waterslide that came out from it that went all the way down the valley.

In the dream, I told her, we went down the slide together. It was wide enough to sit beside each other, so we went down holding hands.

She looked at me, twisting a ring on her finger. It was an engagement ring. We stared at each other, and then she smiled.

"Shut up," she said, laughing, pushing me sideways. "Stop joking around."

I could have told her I was making it up, that I hadn't dreamt this at all. It would have been the time to do so, if I ever had that kind of dream.

The First Hurt

In the doctor's office, back when they used to take X-rays of your feet just to find your shoe size, my grandmother Rose waited for the X-ray machine to begin. She had bad skin and the X-rays were supposed to make whatever it was that made her that way leave. She sat on her hands so she wouldn't pick her face while bright light seeped into her, hiding in her body for years.

Afterward, she could finally bear to trace her profile in the morning light of the yellow tiled bathroom. She met her husband who had planned on marrying her best friend, but her friend didn't love him, so he married Rose instead.

After my grandmother married, only the smallest pieces of skin left her, and after her wedding night, she used her hands to clean the places beneath her bed, to wash the sheets, to vacuum and vacuum, and to spread plates upon the table for dinner.

She was antsy. She was spotless. At night her husband would touch her new skin with the back of his hand.

*

Once my grandmother had skin like mine. She tells me this
and looks at me and says, "A real problem."

She tells me to wash my greasy hair so that it does not rub
the sides of my face at night and taint the pillow while I
dream.

My grandmother moved into our house in the beginning of
September. She took the downstairs guest room for her own
and began to share the best bathroom (the one with the light-
up magnifying mirror) with my mother. Now she can hear
each time I sneak into the room, locking the doors and turning on the bath to steam my face. She has started to knock
now that she knows what I am up to. She bangs with her
small fist.

"Get out of there, Sarah," she says.

I unlock and open the door, letting the hot steam follow me
outside and into the hall. She takes my face into her hands and
puts me close to her mouth.

"Poor thing," she says with chopped-liver breath.

My grandmother had to move in suddenly. She has been
struck by cancer of the bladder: her body has turned on her
and come at her from inside. Now that she is old, she has a
new place to worry about.

When she moved in I helped her unpack. She was neat
with her possessions and had a hard time giving her old
dresses away. But she doesn't like clutter, either. She made
me fold her clothes into tiny squares and then lay them in
crates while she watched from her new bed.

It is October now, and I have gotten into my school routine. It
is a lot like the year before when we first moved here, except

now I know where I can hide and where I can cut through, walking across our property to the old apple orchards past the barking neighbor's dog to get to school. I walk through the woods where the boy's dirt-bike trails leave puddles when it rains, and a small road of leaves and track marks to follow when it is cold.

From where I stand at the edge of the woods, I can see the lacrosse boys who practice all year, out of season, to win championships throughout the state. Where the school fields begin, they do their before-school drills in the early morning. The grass is wet so I squat, hidden by the bare trees that cross over each other. I smoke a cigarette in one hand and a joint in the other. I drink my morning Coke in between puffs.

The lacrosse boys are smooth and blond. Throughout the day they become tougher and when I hear them talk I try not to listen. I like them best in the morning.

The ones that play football interest me less, but they are there too, over to the left on the field, packed into their jock straps and padding that remind me of maxi pads. They are thick necked, and butt with their helmets like bulls. They pound each other's fists and yell in the voice of old frogs. They are boys I would not mind in a large, anonymous soup. But my true loyalty as the most secret of cheerleaders, my silent cheers from the off-the-side sidelines, are always for the lacrosse boys.

"Let them heal," my grandmother says to me at the dinner table, slapping my hand away from my own face. We are all here: my mom, my dad, my grandmother, and me.

"Please leave her alone," my father says, wiping his ugly mustache with his hand.

Rose is my father's mother, so he is gentle with her. My grandmother is fragile, we know, and on her own all day while my parents are at work and I am at school. For the short time we see her each day, we make sure that we are patient, nice.

My grandmother has been here a month. She started to cook for us her first night here. Sometimes I catch her at the sink, looking outside at the old apple orchards that are on our neighbor's property. On the weekends the sounds of the football games seep through our windows.

My grandmother starts cooking when I get home from school. All her food smells similar and usually includes leftovers from the day before.

"Don't let your wet hair dry on your back," my grandmother says.

"Pat your face dry. Don't rub," she says.

She says, "If you do that, you'll get scars."

"Too bad they don't have radiation like they used to," she says. "That would heal you good."

My grandmother does not know what caused her cancer. I am not allowed to tell her what my father told me. He said that those lights on her face—unprotected radiation—might have started the cancer when she was still young. The doctor told him that all those flashes my grandmother thought were burning her bad skin away were actually burning things up inside her. And it might be true.

I always spot him first by his straight-edge shoulders: him. Ham.

Ham is short for Hamilton. Hamilton is a family name. It is a way to name a person without having to think of something new. It is easier to trace the pure breeds this way.

Ham has an anorexic girlfriend named Gretchen who already graduated and is waiting for him to finish his senior year. Gretchen wants to go with him where he goes so she can dirty his new college sink with her water throw-up. She fills the empty space beside him in his Jeep and I imagine her pushing her bony hips up to meet his whenever they are alone.

In the halls when we see each other, Ham nods and winks and smiles at me. In last period art class, at the back table where we sit together, Ham draws Led Zeppelin covers, boats on docks, and Grateful Dead skeletons with hats. I am working on a drawing of a dream I had of a woman in a blue bonnet looking up from the bottom of a lake. I swim above her rotting face.

After the bell rings and before his after-school practice starts, Ham and I walk into the woods and deep into the bike trails to smoke. Ham leans in to light my joint or cigarette. My army jacket rubs against him just a little. After a few puffs, his blue eyes turn soft and fly into the tops of the trees. I always think how I would like to lie down and look at the clouds that cover us, to stare at the sky that passes the boats at night so that the water looks like a bay of milk from the country-club lights, and then to imagine the horizon that sweeps out of here and escapes, falling off the land and reflecting the sea.

"Gretchen is getting thinner," Ham tells me one day when we have skipped art class all together. "I try to make her eat . . ."

Gretchen is all bones. When she comes to pick him up from practice in her own black Jeep, her rooted blonde hair looks stringy and sick. It is hard for me to feel sad for her since last year, when I was new, Gretchen was one of the girls who would giggle with her friends from the last stall of the girl's room when I came in. She made fun of me, whispering things in a loud whisper, things like "smell" and "zit."

"I'm sorry," I say.

The coach's whistle blows and Ham takes one more puff.

"Hey, thanks again," Ham says. He knows I always have weed.

After a night's first series of picking I steam my face in a tin cooking pot full of boiling water. I cover the back of my head with a towel so that the steam won't get out. I put cold washcloths on afterward and lie in bed.

Under the covers, I take myself past the playing fields across the mist and goalie posts and bleachers and equipment sheds. I take myself out and into the red doors of the boy's locker room.

Each boy inside has his very own locker. Some are hung with towels and some have pictures of girls and rock bands. Some are empty and some sport deodorant. Each has a lock with its very own code.

I like to think about these boys not thinking about me as I hover. I watch their backs that lean onto the ribs, which are held up by the pectorals (or so it seems), supporting the necks and pretty faces they keep rosy all year.

"Do you have any friends?" my grandmother asks me while I eat canned pears out of the can after school.

"Why don't you join a sport?" she asks.

My grandmother makes me go with her to the mall so she can buy new "hose." She drives fast, not like other grandmothers, and she parks near the entrance so she will not have to walk far.

"You don't have to come with me, honey," she says. "Why don't you look at some dresses and I'll meet you? Maybe you can try on some nice clothes."

I leave my grandmother and walk past the makeup counters, where I am sure the makeup women are dying to cover my bad skin up, and to the women's section. I walk around the fancy dresses, touching the sequins, then I go to the furs.

"May I help you?" a woman asks, and I quickly take my hand off the mink I had been petting.

"No, no," I say. I look up; the saleswoman is Gretchen.

I did not know Gretchen sold furs.

"Hey," she says, "didn't you go to North?"

"Yes," I say, "I still do."

"I thought so," she says. She doesn't smile.

"Ham is your boyfriend," I say.

Gretchen is so thin she looks like she could get lost here, falling somewhere inside a coat, the same size as the skeleton of the animal the fur is made of. Inside the coat, no one would ever find her.

Gretchen's lips are dry.

"Yes," she says, "you know him?"

"Yup," I say, and realize that I am not part of any conversation Gretchen and Ham have ever had.

"Sarah," I hear my grandmother's voice calling.

"Coming," I say, but my grandmother is already behind me; her bony hand presses onto my back.

"Oh, hello!" my grandmother says.

"Goodbye, Gretchen," I say, taking my grandmother's hand and leading her away.

"Do you know her?" my grandmother asks. "Why don't you introduce me to your friend?"

*

I love when Ham drives, stick shifting down, cigarette in his other hand, hair still wet from his shower.

The plastic windows of Ham's Jeep flap against the bars while he drives us to his members-only country club.

He parks in the lot and I follow him down to the beach. The moon and the safety lights reflect off the water. It is cold but nice out and I like the feel of my sneakers sinking into the sand.

We sit and I take out a bag of weed.

"I saw Gretchen," I say.

Ham's eyes look away from the weed and at me.

"At the mall, in the fur department," I tell him.

"Yeah, she's just doing that until I graduate. Then we'll probably go to school near each other," he says, looking back down.

"Oh," I say.

"But it's kind of a secret that she is working there. Even her friends don't know," he says.

"Uh-huh," I say.

"Yeah, so don't say anything, okay?"

"Yup," I say.

I wish I could lay my secrets down and pick away the ones I didn't have to keep. I would tell everyone about Gretchen and the furs and I would tell Ham that I loved him.

Ham faces away from the wind and rolls a fat joint.

"Nice," he says, lighting it and taking a drag.

I separate out his portion from my own. We go back and forth with the joint taking hits. It turns soft from our spit right there on the joint that I hold with my fingers: his spit and mine. Wet.

*

My grandmother tells me that my grandfather cheated.

She holds my hand. She is always touching me.

"All men cheat," she says.

We sit on the couch after school. Already it is turning dark out. It is the worst time of the day.

Outside are whole bags filled with leaves that the trash man picks up. Leaves gone until the next week when Connor, whose father lost his job for being a drunk and now teaches driver's ed, rakes.

Since my grandmother has moved in, the house is always clean. She folds tissues and puts them next to her bed. In the living room, we sit on the berber carpet and fold laundry together. We watch Connor out the window.

"So, do you have a boyfriend?" my grandmother asks, putting one sock into another.

"No," I say, wondering why she would ask me after telling me that men were all bad.

"You will," she says.

I look at Connor, raking my lawn; a boy who does not talk to me in class, or even look at me in the halls. It is like it is our secret: he rakes my family's leaves.

I fold my mother's bra, my father's jockeys. I look out the window where Connor ties up a full plastic bag.

"I'm not . . ." I say.

"I know," my grandmother says, reaching across the laundry basket to touch my arm. She knows about men and she knows they do not want me. And I don't even remember what I was going to say.

We have been picked to paint the mural outside the classroom. We sit in class and try to brainstorm.

"How about, like, the Led Zeppelin poster of all those naked kids climbing up the mountain?" Ham says.

I laugh.

"Okay, then, what do you want to do?"

While we brainstorm, I am secretly drawing Ham while Ham draws a marijuana plant with tears dripping from its leaves.

"Who's that?" he asks, trying to see my drawing.

"A boy," I say.

"What boy?" he asks.

"One of them," I tell him. I have wanted to paint the wall of my room red for a long time, but haven't. I have a sketchbook where I have copied all of my favorite boys from the yearbook, but I do not want to share that.

My grandmother has only seen me from my neck up. She has never even caught a peek of my terrain of secret skin. On my chest, my back, my arms, I have things growing at the base of me that only I can feel the first hurt of.

I sit on my bed and pick the skin on my thighs. Once you start to touch somewhere, new things come up, because you have been picking. You can find a place on your body you never thought of and just start touching it, scratching it. Soon there will be bumps. I promise.

It's like magic: you touch your skin with the things you were given—hands and oil and pores. All you are doing is wiping yourself with love.

He picks me up and we drive to his beach club. It is night again, and we sit on the sand, cupping our hands so that the joint stays lit.

Ham points to where he docks his boat in the summer and then points to his family's cabana.

I watch him blow the smoke and wonder where Gretchen is.

"Nice," Ham says, nodding and breathing out.

"Thanks," I say, like I made the pot, like I am one of those mothers who say thank you when you tell them their kid is cute.

"Hey, wait a second," Ham says, and runs to his car. He comes back with a six-pack. "I was supposed to meet up with some guys, but I'm feeling chill."

Ham takes out his lighter and pops open two beers, and I sip even though I don't really like it. I drink fast, and Ham watches me.

"Whoa, girl," he says, but then he tips his own beer back and I watch his Adam's apple go up and down, gurgling the beer until it is gone. I wonder why boys have Adam's apples. Biologically I can't think of why. But I like them anyway.

Suddenly, Ham's face is in front of me. He leans in but then exhales his smoke into my mouth.

"Ha," he laughs, as I swallow the smoke and cough. "You ever do that before?"

"No," I say.

"Two for one, see?" he says.

I do it back to him, making sure it doesn't seem like I am trying to make our lips touch.

"If you close the hole you get all of it," he says, meaning to close the hole, the space between us, the space between his lips and mine.

We do that, and it is like kissing.

We both start laughing.

"Gretchen wouldn't like that," I say, wiping my mouth.

"She smokes with me like that sometimes," he says.

I don't explain. I look out onto the water where the boys sail in the summertime.

*

They announce over the speakers that all practice will be called off today because of the rain.

"Cool," Ham says. "Let's go smoke. Gretchen's working today."

We get out of class early by asking to go to the bathroom. We meet up and walk across the field with our jackets over our heads to the dirt-bike trails in the woods. I lead him back into the woods where there is a tire swing hanging from one of the tallest trees.

Ham jumps up and secures his feet in the tire, leaning back to start himself going. He swings while I watch from the mud, puffing quickly on the perfect joint he rolled with my dollar.

"This is awesome," he yells.

He wears jeans that are low and a T-shirt and a parka. His blond hair blows away from his face when he comes toward me and forward when he flies back.

"Push me higher," Ham says.

I put out the joint on the bark of a tree and put it in my cigarette case for later. I start pushing, only touching the swing. It isn't raining so hard in the woods since the leaves of the highest trees are like a roof. Or like a tundra.

"Isn't it like a tundra up there?" I yell up to him. I am stoned.

"What? You mean like an ecosystem?" he asks.

"Kind of," I say.

"You're weird," he says, holding his hand out to stop me from pushing, dragging his sneaker on the dirt to stop himself.

"How am I weird?" I ask.

I wait for his answer but instead he growls. His foot seems to bend under itself so that his ankle touches the ground. Ham falls forward over the top of the tire.

"Fuck!" he yells. His sneaker is covered in mud.

I run over to him. "Are you okay?" I ask.

"I think I sprained my fucking ankle! Fuck! I can't believe this!"

Ham has fallen back now and is sitting in the dirt, the hurt foot held up by the inside of the tire like a sling.

Ham squints his eyes and leans over in pain.

"Should I get someone?" I ask him.

He breathes in and out in big long breaths. I wish I were a physical therapist so I could tell him that all his pain is centered in his stomach. I would pull up his shirt to look at his chest and press on it with my hands, telling him to breathe in and out.

He shakes his head from side to side and pats the ground beside him. He lies his head in the dirty leaves.

"Just take my foot out of here," he says, "please."

I hold Ham's running foot, his walking through the halls and stopping right outside the classroom so his sneakers squeak foot. I hold his standing foot that he sometimes pushes up to the tiptoe while fucking Gretchen on the bathroom sink, or just holding her, because she is so light, up against the mirror of his parent's bedroom. I hold the foot that sometimes kicks me beneath the art-room table to show me the big bud he has hidden in his pocket. This foot, his admission to schools with lacrosse teams foot, is in my hands.

I gently pull the swing out and bring his foot to the ground. I untie his laces slowly while he watches and slip off the shoe. I pull the tip of the top of his sock and put my finger in the elastic where I can feel the small blond ankle hairs that are matted down with sweat. Holding both the top of the sock and the toe of the sock, I inch it off of him. Ham's foot is red and swollen.

We lie side by side and look at the top of the trees. It has stopped raining and I can hear only the trickle of the old rain trying to find its way down through the leaves. I look over at Ham's face. There is wetness at the corner of his eye.

"I just want to wait a little longer, okay?" he asks.

I nod. I have always wanted this.

"Imagine someone finds us here," he says.

I begin to pick my face. By this time I would usually be home, locked in the bathroom while my grandmother started her defrosting. I would have already scouted the day's new growths, beginning with my face and then going down to my chest and my back. I would have wiped the condensation off the mirror with my mother's towel.

I can feel Ham looking at me while I pick my face. I can feel that I am bleeding in little dots and I swipe the sleeve of my sweater across my cheek.

"Why do you do that?" he asks.

I shrug and tell him because I am bored.

"Why don't you try a sport then?" he asks.

"Fuck you," I say.

"I'm trying to help you, Sarah," Ham says.

"You don't know how to help me," I say.

I get up and stand above him.

"What do you mean?" he asks.

"Nothing," I say. I kick leaves on his chest.

"Kick a man when he's down," Ham says, trying to smile.

"Whatever," I say.

Suddenly I hear the sound of dirt bikes getting louder and louder. Ham uses his arms to sit. Then he reaches up for me. The dirt bike sounds get louder but I cannot see them yet.

They go over the trails they have left before. They come back like dogs, sniffing the same territory.

The dirt bikers pull off their helmets and I recognize them from school.

"Hey, Ham," one of them says. "What happened?"

"I'm hurt," Ham says, trying to turn his neck to see them.

"He fell off the tire swing," I tell them.

Two of the dirt bikers lean down to pick him up. They are not jocks, but they are boys, and they seat him on the back of the biggest bike, pulling his good foot over first like a child in a car seat.

The one from my math class gets on in front of Ham. He revs his engine.

"Hold on," he yells back to Ham.

Ham looks pale while they drive away. He holds the biker around his waist, his head leaning on the biker's back. His eyes are closed and puffy and his bad foot is naked and still swelling. I hold his shoe and sock and then throw them toward the tire swing while the bikers drive away. The sneaker goes through the circle of the tire and the sock flops to the ground.

Sports.

My grandmother is sitting at the kitchen table cutting oranges.

"Sarah," she says. "Why are you so late?"

I sit down next to her and pick up one of the wedges beneath her knife and fingers.

"Careful!" she says, slapping my hand away.

I put the orange in my mouth and suck, making noise. The juice is good.

"Do you want some more?" she asks, getting up to put them on a plate.

"No," I say.

My grandmother takes an orange wedge and puts it inside her mouth and sucks it.

I laugh, and she takes the orange out and puts her dry, freckled hand on my cheek. I look down at her other hand resting on her bony knees, her finger swollen around her old wedding ring.

"It will be okay," she says, rubbing her finger back and forth along my bumps.

I do not want to talk, so I cry into her belly while she pats my back.

She whispers, her breath strong in my ear, "Someday you'll have skin like mine."

Homestay

Welcome

This year, like every year, you are blonde. This year: lavender. We spot you at the airport by the lavender sweater you have wrapped around your shoulders.

We show you your basement room with its cheap, argyle-print carpet where you will sleep on a hard, double mattress. We have built you a shower whose head trickles water down only after we have all finished showering. You wash yourself less, we figure: you are from Denmark.

We know by now that you will not shave the down beneath your arms. We know that you will pluck the hairs on your legs without a wastebasket beside you in our living room. You will let the small, stiff hairs fall onto the white carpet, where they will hide like ants until your next vacuuming.

Housing

My father hears noises coming from the basement when he comes home late. We are all asleep except for you and him.

My mother is lucky that blondes are not his type. Still, she will buy you a bathrobe on your first Hanukkah to cover yourself up—until then you only wear short shirts and underwear to breakfast.

"It's different in Denmark," my mother says.

For dinner you make meatballs and potatoes until my father says something.

You take your top off at the beach club until my father says something.

When my father hears the noises, he opens the first set of folding doors that mark off my parents' section of the house. He closes the doors behind him, then takes off his shoes in the study. He does not wake my mother.

In my parents' room, lying in the dark, my father still hears your sounds. He hears you clearly now—our house was made cheaply, with thin walls and ceilings, by an airplane pilot for his family.

My father hears you crying but he does not get up. You, he knows, are not his type.

Upstairs from my father I am dreaming of kittens, sick and locked in the trunk of a car.

Privacy

You are dangerous. You could walk in anytime. You are one more person in our small, weak house.

You are blonde. You are pretty. I brush your hair and knock on your door in the morning to look at your closet of clothes.

You are Christian. You are Danish. You have only seen what it is like to be American in our house.

You are dangerous. You are one more person in our home. You could twist my doorknob so that it opens, even when it is locked.

Location

We live on the island at the beginning of a cul-de-sac. From where we are you can hear the school sports teams practice after school. We can hear the cheering from the stands on weekends and boys making paths with their dirt bikes, driving through the woods that separate our lawn from the school field.

We live near the water. We can drive from our house to the causeway that runs through the bay and the sound, leading out to the neck of the island.

When it snows, the causeway is closed. When it snows, you will be glad you are here.

At our house, on snow days, we will unfold the blankets and eat defrosted bagels on the floor of the living room. We will stay in our pajamas all day.

I will pick the dandruff from your scalp, and we will look out the window at my father's disappearing yard.

The water will start to freeze and the snow that will cover the golf course, the school gym, the beach club, and the tennis courts, will also cover the shore. Soon we will not be able to tell where the land stops and the water begins.

Pay and Privileges

Sixty dollars a week plus free boarding plus use of a car plus travel time plus a family waiting to be all yours for a year. For a whole year you will be the only Danish person in our house.

Please remember there are other girls with your name waiting in a pile of postcards in my mother's top, desk drawer. We have kept their photos, which I sneak in her desk to look at. The ones who look like you I put away. The other ones, the ones without luck, I bring up to my room and put in a box marked "Girls."

Responsibilities

1. To help me get up after I faint in the shower. I haven't eaten enough and have been screaming your name from the second-floor bathroom, yelling at you when you do not come fast enough.

2. To run from the sunken living room, where you have been reading a magazine, past the dining room and up the staircase. My mother has hung pictures of our family that I will soon knock down, sweeping my arm against the wall and watching people with my face fall on each stair. I break their frames, which I will have to clean up.

3. To watch me pick up tiny bits of glass from inside the carpet, cutting my fingers. I will have to pay for new picture frames with the money I earn from working in a French pastry shop. I refuse to describe the cakes and pastries to the customers; the words "chewy" and "moist" make me sick.

4. To open the door without knocking and turn off the water when you get to the upstairs bathroom. Inside, you feel the heat from the red heat lamps on your sweater, through your shirt. You find me, without a towel, lying on the floor of the bathtub, still yelling your name.

Holidays

At Christmas, in your home, you have a large Christmas tree. You give out your presents on Christmas Eve and dance in a circle around the tree. You wear funny hats and drink.

"Skol!" you say, lifting your glasses and pouring more.

You have those features: small stubby fingers, short hands, a pushed-in nose. Your mother must have been drinking while you were inside her. Or else you have a mother with small stubby fingers, short hands, and a pushed-in nose. Or a father. Or a mother that had a mother who drank too.

Vacations

My parents drive the car north for hours. You are stuck in the backseat with my doll and me. I am too old to have a doll. You watch me smell my fingers on my left hand.

The doll is in the shape of me. It is me in the world of dolls. It has black yarn hair and black button eyes. In the doll world, my skin is the color of cotton balls.

When we get there, it is dark. Inside the small, wood house, bare lightbulbs light the rooms. There are wood beams holding up the second floor. You and I must share a room.

"There's a lake," my mother says.

It is late. Out the window of our room we can see the black lake water. We think we see canoes, a buoy, a painted dock, and a bicycle lying flat on the sand.

We are tired and get into bed with my doll, which I keep on my side. Your T-shirt rides up your back when you lie down. I do not wear underwear to sleep.

Midnight, you can hear me. I am loving my doll. I have turned her sideways so that her hip is pointed. I shake the bed with my love. I am arched like a dolphin, moving sideways, on top. I have made no space between my doll and me, so that when I move, we all move together.

Transportation

Twice a week you drive me across the island. You drop me off at the bottom of a driveway, watch me walk onto the blacktop, up the hill, and in the side door of a large white house. You drive away and pick up roast beef sandwiches and french fries and biscuits. You eat your dinner and bring me mine.

Fifty minutes later you are back at the bottom of the driveway. I come out, walking quickly down the blacktop, and get in the passenger door. I have small eyes that look pruned on the sides.

"Here," you say. You hand me my dinner.

"Thank you," I say. I eat while you drive.

We turn on the radio. I eat each thing separately.

My mother has tried to explain analysis to you before, but in Denmark, it is only for crazies.

"Here," my mother has told you, "everyone goes."

You do not ask me what I talk about in the white house. You do not ask me what I am thinking. You do not have an office with modern furniture and a picture of two camels intertwined on the wall. You do not lean back in your black leather chair and stare at me and smile. Instead you stare ahead and drive. Still, I tell you my dreams on the car ride home.

Free Time

There are other au pairs. My mother and her friends brought them over at the same time. All the girls are from Denmark. Each of my mother's friends is also a mother, and each of her friends has a girl of her own.

On the patio, I can hear the mothers talking:

"I came home the other day and the kids were all inside, alone, while she was outside smoking."

"I didn't know she would be so cute. I mean, her picture did NOT do her justice."

"I couldn't believe she didn't set the alarm. I reminded her three times the night before, and she still forgot to set it."

"I said, 'dressy' and she came down wearing a halter top and jeans!"

"Can you understand yours? How am I supposed to understand mine?"

"You can always send her back."

"You can always get another one."

"There's always next year's."

"We could trade."

Family Life

I spy on you and my father in the living room, late. You are both drinking from the kiddush cups my mother's father gave us. It is not Shabbos, and you are not drinking wine.

My father, who once made you cry, lifts up his metal glass and toasts you.

"L'Chaim," he says.

The glasses make a metal sound.

You smile and say, "I didn't know you liked this stuff."

My father makes a face when swallowing.

"I don't," he says, still in his work suit and tie.

My father laughs, "I don't like it at all."

Miscellaneous

Eva . . . Tina . . . Lena . . . Seena . . . Bettina . . . Christina . . .
We may call you last year's name. You are from the world of
Legoland. We know: you have shown us pictures.

You show us pictures of your father in his Christmas
sweater. Your brother Christian wears a shiny soccer outfit.
Your mother smiles and holds your dog.

In Denmark it gets dark in the winter. An entire season
paints your windows black.

You soak up the sun here. Each day you wake to light. I
wonder if this throws some cycle of yours off. Are you men-
struating normally? Are things off-kilter? Is the tilt of the
earth, the change of the weather, turning you inside out?

Length of Stay

You have left the letter on my bed. You have written my name on the outside of the envelope. I recognize my mother's stationery with its tiny blue pattern.

My mother calls my name from downstairs. I can hear her cursing, scuffing the kitchen floor with her shoes.

I open the letter. It is sealed with tape, not spit. I wonder if this is the Danish way: to leave without a trace.

You have not been with us long enough to see all of America. You have not even been here long enough to see me grow. But you are leaving, your letter says. By now you are gone.

I remember that you owe my father money. Will you pay it back?

My mother calls my name from the kitchen.

I look in my box and find my pictures. I line them up to pick: girls all in a row.

I figure there is only so much you wanted to see of our family. And Denmark waits for you, its blond wood tables shimmering.

I keep your letter. My mother throws your photo away.

Together my mother and I sort through the postcards. We each pick a girl with your hair. Then I give her my girl, and she hands me hers.

Keeping Time

Bunk K is made of logs and screens and filled with eleven-year-old girls. These girls still wake up easily and early; they do not wear deodorant yet. They are still lithe, still children, and pretty, still, in an undeveloped way. I am their counselor, and sometimes they watch me in the shower.

My co-counselor, Wendy, is chubby and silly and the girls like her too. But I am the one they sit up for in their pj's way after lights out. I am the one that brings the chilly, beer-filled air in from outside to listen to my girls.

"What were you doing?" they whisper. "Where have you been?"

On the first Friday of camp we sit Indian-style on the wood floor of our bunk. Walking inside the circle of girls, I pour M&M's into each set of small, cupped hands.

"Oh, I know this game," Janet says. She is a camp veteran, here the year before.

"Well, let's try it again," I say. "Don't eat them yet."

The "get-to-know-you" game is simple: Eat one M&M for each thing you tell about yourself.

Red is for love. The girls love chocolate and swimming and pets. Love is easy.

Green is for hate.

"I hate Easter Bunnies," April, a girl whose hair has never been cut, says and swallows.

Colleen hates snakes and Jenny M. hates butter and Alex and Jenny B. both hate having to go to the bathroom in the woods on campouts.

There are two girls with braces who hate them. I hate circuses.

"I hate liars," Trisha, the skinny girl with the whitest skin in the bunk, says. She tells us she also hates the sun. I decide, after this first full week of camp, that she is my favorite. My favorite because of her glasses that make her eyes look bigger than they are, and her skinny legs and one-piece bathing suits; my favorite because she will tread water by the diving board the entire swim time just to talk to me; my favorite because in a few days she will tell me I should take my underwear off to sleep so that my vagina can "breathe."

"Let's do red again!" someone says. We go back to loving.

When it is my turn I say I love pearls.

"What about Chris?" Trisha asks, looking at a brown M&M that she has balanced on her pointer finger.

"Yeah, what about Chris?" the other girls echo.

I look over at fat Wendy who smiles.

I have the urge to make them wait until nighttime and then put a flashlight under my face. Part of me wants to tell them about Chris, the cute counselor I won during counselor training week by teaming up with him in volleyball. That during the day, when Chris is a counselor for the boy's bunk B, he is thinking about what he does at night. During the school year Chris goes to a good college because he played lacrosse. In the dawn Chris is a dreamer who forgets his dreams in the morning.

I wanted to tell the girls, while they sat Indian-style on the floor in their pajama tops and bottoms, that Chris, the boy everyone loved, unbuttoned his shorts and pulled himself out while I lay on my back and watched in the back of his van. I watched him watch me while he touched himself; I watched his blond hair begin to stick to his forehead from sweat.

I listened to the sound of his palm against himself, against his shorts. When he came I watched his face, watched him close his eyes and giggle, watched him as he lay back down on top of me, getting my stomach wet. He kissed me, smiling and embarrassed, lighting a joint and passing it over.

During the day I keep time. It is my job all day long. I watch the girls with one eye while I sit on the edge of the diving board, swinging my legs back and forth.

When their time is finally up, I blow my whistle and put my hands above my head. I motion for the girls with water-logged ears and the girls who are still underwater: those lucky girls who see me blurry from underneath, lost in the only good sound.

My second night off, I put the girls to bed and make sure that Wendy is okay. I finish my job and meet Chris at the pool.

It is dark and he is naked, already swimming without me. I watch him look up at the sky.

I go up to the rim of the pool and splash water on his stomach with my foot.

"Come in," he says, smiling, swimming to the edge of the pool where I am standing. He holds onto my ankles with his wet hands.

"Come in," he says, looking up at me.

Even though it is chilly, his wet hands feel good.

"Come on," he says, stroking my shins.

I feel like a man the way I want him. It is sad the way I want him. But I look past him, over him. I feel myself in the air above him when I dive in.

Afterward, I would answer the girls' questions. One at a time I would point to their small, raised hands, their fingernails polished with my only bottle of nail polish left. Each girl in my bunk has red lacquered nails, slowly chipping away with each day in the lake or the pool. I would even let fat Wendy ask me questions: fat Wendy who I found one night with her pillow between her legs and her head pushed against the thin mattress, shaking the springs.

Colleen would raise her hand first.

"Was it big?" she would ask when I called on her. No one would laugh because Colleen is popular.

"Yes," I would say, holding out my hands to show the length of a hammer, then closing the space slowly, trying to remember if it was really that large.

"Was it sticky?" Trisha would ask, and all the girls would giggle.

"Yes," I would say, "it got on his pants. He was trying to be gentle and trying to concentrate."

"Someday," I would say, "you'll get to look in a boy's eyes when he surprises himself."

I would tell my girls, "It is something to see."

During free time we sit on the bunks writing letters, making string bracelets, playing games.

Trisha sits on my bottom bunk and braids my hair. Her small fingers touch me behind my ears and on my neck.

"I saw you and Chris," she whispers.

The bunk—the girls—seems to get even smaller. I close my eyes and feel my face get hot then cold. I do not move, but my neck sweats beneath her breath.

"Where?" I ask, still looking forward so she cannot see my face. "When?"

"In the sand, by the lake," she says. "Wendy took me to the infirmary on your night off and I saw you."

"Do you know Chris?" I ask.

"Of course! He's my volleyball instructor," she says.

"Did Wendy see too?" I whisper.

"No," Trisha says, finishing the braid and wrapping the elastic around the bottom. She snaps the last band against my hair and pats my head.

"Just me," she says.

Trisha sits next to me on the diving board. She has white sunblock striped down her nose, and freckles on either side of it. She tells me about her new canopy bed at home and her mom who is a social worker and has an office attached to the side of her house. She tells me how she was going to have a little brother or sister but then her mom had a miscarriage.

"Look! It's Chris!" she says, pointing toward the gate of the pool.

We both watch as Chris walks toward us, waving to the girls like a rock star.

"Hi, Chris," Trisha says. She runs to him and he picks her up and hangs her upside down while he walks over to me.

"I got a live one here," he says, flipping her over and poking her in the belly button of her one-piece. Then, picking her up by the armpits, he throws her in the pool.

"No!" she yells, just before the water hits. He laughs and watches her splash, then he sits next to me on the diving board. I watch as Trisha swims to the other end of the pool and holds on to the far edge to watch us.

"How's it going?" I ask.

"Oh, just resting with the boys down by the flagpole," he says, touching my fingers with his pinkie so no one can see.

I want to listen to the sound of the girls with my eyes closed.

He puts his finger in the crease of my palm and whispers, "I wish I could fuck you right now."

I close my eyes for just one second, and hope no one is drowning.

I look down and Trisha is treading water beneath us. I take my hand back from Chris.

"I think swim time is over," she says, her teeth chattering.

I put my whistle in my mouth and look at my watch.

"It's time," I say, standing up and putting my arms over my head, then exhaling hard into my whistle. I watch the girls until they are all out of the water and safe. Then I blow the whistle again for lineup and watch as Chris walks out of the gate. The girls stand inside their towels with blue lips and puddles beneath them. They wait for me to lead them to where they are supposed to go.

Chris and I sit in the woods on a stiff, green camp blanket.

"You know," I say, "Trisha saw us."

"When?" he asks.

"The other night. When we were on the sand."

He laughs, "Maybe she learned something!"

"Shut up," I say, pushing him over. I take a swig of the cheap wine he brought.

"She's my favorite," I tell him.

"I thought I was," he says.

We drink more wine and touch hands and make love. I want to feel the way I do when I watch the girls fight or talk or sleep. I want to feel the way I do when I think of them growing. I want to feel that way when Chris kisses me with his eyes closed while I watch him. He has done nothing wrong.

Afterward I lie on his chest and he lies on his back. He looks at the sky and I look at his chest. We breathe together and I wish I could look at the sky too.

"I forgot to tell you," he says.

He strokes my head. I remember how I used to think when boys did things like that it meant love.

"What?" I ask.

"Well, I didn't forget. But I wanted to tell you. I've decided to be the groundskeeper here during the year."

I pick my head up to look at him.

"Really?" I ask. "What about school?"

He is looking at me with a serious face.

"Well, they need someone up here year round, and I quit school. I quit in the spring. Plus, up here I can go skiing . . . "

After camp I am going back to my life. I am going back upstate to my college where I have a dorm room with a futon and a guy down the hall I sometimes sleep with. I am signed up for two lit classes, a math requirement, and a gender-studies class called "Gender, Patronage, and the Decorative Arts in the Renaissance." I am already talking with friends about a trip to Aruba during winter break.

"Aren't you going to be bored?" I ask.

"Well, I don't know. I don't really have a choice. I mean, the truth is, I got kicked out. Grades and stuff. Bullshit. But I think it's going to be awesome up here, you know? All alone in the wilderness. I think it will be awesome to be the only one here."

I imagine him a skinny wolf-boy, growing hair all winter and running naked through the girls' bunks, tearing the mattresses with his teeth.

"I don't know what to say," I tell him.

"Say you'll visit me," he says, squeezing my hand.

I put my head back on the blanket and look at the sky. I imagine the snow on top of the mud and the sand. Snow that will help start the dirt to get ready for next year's girls to grow on. There was no point to camp when there was no one to keep track of.

"What?" he says. "It's no big deal."

I can see that Chris is trying to smile. I put my finger to his bony nose.

"I know," I say, and we go back to kissing.

In the water, the girls pull at my legs and shoulders, dunking me under. The girls are rowdy today: the summer dance was announced in the mess hall last night.

Now it is time for dates. It is time for notes thrown from boy to girl: notes flung in the shape of planes across the mess hall. It is time for counselors to relay messages from one camper to another. Campers mouth to each other at bonfire "yes" with a smile. Or they make their best friends mouth "no" while they look the other way.

Trisha sits in the sand. She has her usual traces of white sunscreen on her nose and neck. I wave to her from the water, smiling while I am dunked by the other girls. This mess of girls pushes me beneath dirty lake water where there are green weeds and other things I do not want to see.

I swim away from them as fast as I can toward the shore. I wonder what these girls will be like one day. I have gotten them at the beginning of their stories, when all they have are buds for nipples, little crushes, and waists so small that their towels wrap around them three times. I want to know how they will end up. I want to know who in the group will turn ugly. Who will end up a worrier, and who will end up a slut? I want to know who will turn out like one of the other counselors. Who will turn out like me?

I get out of the lake and lie down next to Trisha on my towel.

"I don't have a date!" Trisha says. She looks at me, her green eyes behind her glasses. Then she lies on her stomach and puts her face in her palms. I reach out to pat her back but she flinches away. Some nights I've watched her sleep.

"Not everyone has a date, Trisha," I say, and wish I hadn't said her name. We both know I am lying.

Trisha is right. Everyone has a date except for her.

Suddenly I feel wetness and weight on my back: one slick body after another—a pile of wet girls—fall upon me. Beneath them I am trapped on my towel, pressed against the sand.

They giggle and crush me, then tickle me until I scream "Mercy!" Finally, they slowly dismount. I can feel the shift of weight as each girl leaves. When the last one stands I feel a new, cold breeze.

Chris has suddenly appeared and I watch as Trisha wiggles in his lap. Chris is tickling her, trapping her. Her eyes are closed; her mouth is open. Her face has the feeling I wish I had when Chris touches me.

The girls get ready for the dance. They have washed their hair the night before and braided it so that today it is wavy. Colleen has an aqua-blue eye pencil and the girls line up so she can draw around their eyes.

"How do I look?" they all ask, trying and retrying different outfits that they trade each other and then give each other back.

Trisha sits on my bed. She is wearing white shorts and sandals and my white tank top with small pink flowers on it. I wore it with Chris last night—it is dirty and smells like me—but Trisha insists on it.

Outside the mess hall, the girls start whispering and giggling. The boys punch each other and laugh too.

Colleen goes right up to her date—a boy who has those rosy cheeks that can make boys look beautiful. She kisses him, straight on the mouth.

Chris stands next to his boys. He looks especially attractive in the nice light. It makes everything whiter, just before it gets dark. His teeth glow when he smiles at me.

When all the bunks have arrived we start lining up to get in. Trisha holds one of my hands and Chris, secretly, rubs his pinkie in my palm.

"What a beautiful shirt," Chris says to Trisha. He leans over and pokes her in the belly of my tank top where his hand touched my stomach last night.

Trisha giggles. She is not a giggler.

"You gonna dance with me?" Chris asks her.

Trisha smiles and blushes.

"Yes," she answers, quietly. It is almost a whisper.

Inside the mess hall it is dark with balloons and music and punch. Some of the older girls are already in the middle of the dance floor, all doing the same dance.

Some kids hit balloons back and forth. Some of the younger boys run around the room, touching the walls, making bases. Slow songs start and couples pair off.

I grab some M&M's from the snack table and Trisha and I play on one side of me, while Chris and I poke each other in the ribs on the other.

I pick up a red M&M and say to Trisha, "I love camp."

"See the kid with the high-tops?" Chris says. "That's the one I caught masturbating."

He points out one boy's hand on another girl's ass and laughs.

Chris will be cleaning this floor in a month, and there will be nothing to laugh at.

I look back to Trisha as she picks a green.

"I hate camp," she says.

I pick red again. "Bunk K," I say.

Trisha pops a green one and chews while she says, "Breakfast." She kicks the legs of her chair.

"You better ask her," I whisper to Chris. "You promised."

"Yeah," he says, smiling and leaning over me, putting out his hand to my girl and asking, "Ready?"

Again Trisha blushes. She steals a red one from my palm.

"Yes," she says, and takes Chris's hand.

I watch as they dance to a fast song. Trisha's skinny legs try to keep a beat. Chris dances like boys do and holds her hands and twirls her around and around.

He looks over at me and makes silly faces while Trisha concentrates on her turns.

A slow song comes on. I want to butt in on either of them. I want to dance.

Chris picks Trisha up by her armpits and she puts her legs around his waist. He spins around with her straddling him while she leans her head back, laughing.

I see some of the other girls, looking over their boyfriend's shoulder to watch as Trisha holds on. She puts both arms around his neck, her head on his shoulder, and Chris takes his arms away, looks at me, laughs, and shrugs.

On the sidelines, I am laughing too.

I alternate my M&M's, then eat them.

Green: mowing my father's lawn.

Red: the pool.

Green: chapped elbows.

Red: my white tank top with its tiny pink flowers.

The song begins to fade, mixing into the next song, which is fast. I get up from my seat so Chris can twirl us both around.

Chris takes Trisha under her arms to put her down but she holds on and puts one hand on his face. They look at each other, and then she leans in. She kisses him on the lips, softly, a second too long.

I watch him forget everything and then remember as he drops her down and pushes her onto the hardwood floor. He wipes his mouth with his hand, then runs to the screen doors of the mess hall, pushing them open and running out.

Everyone looks. The mess hall doors slam. The music stays beating: oblivious.

Trisha is on the floor, looking up at the ceiling. Her tears drip down the sides of her face but she does not wipe them away. I watch as Wendy and the other counselors run to her while I stay frozen. They huddle around her, making a counselor tent. I watch and stand. Then I run out the screen doors.

Camp might be the meanest thing you can do to a child. Especially if your counselor runs after her boyfriend instead of holding you. Especially if you are the smallest, palest girl in the bunk and you have seen something you should not have seen.

Especially if, after leaving your parents, all you want is a kiss.

"Chris!" I yell and run outside, "Chris!"

I run toward the lake to him because no one else is, I tell myself. It is better to be at camp with someone than to be alone.

I find him in the water, splashing his face with his hands, still wearing all his clothes.

I dive in and when I am deep enough I swim to him.

Chris and I get deep enough so that only our heads are above water. I can tell that he is crying.

"It's okay," I say, trying to reach out and touch him.

"I don't know why I'm fucking crying," he says. He rubs his eyes and tries to smile.

Chris kisses me while underwater there are things I do not want to see.

He says my name, and I straddle his legs while he holds me up. I lean back to float and look up at the dark sky.

We can hear the dance still going on. The sting of what has happened is still there, but the counselors whisper and smile, hoping the kids will be distracted by the music and the punch.

I let Chris carry me out of the water and put me on the sand. I sit up and look back at the mess hall, the colored balloons tied to the railing: oblivious.

The balloons are pink and yellow and white. They are girl's colors that stand for nothing. They are the colors in between.

Yellow is the feeling of hitting the blond wood that is forever worn from summers of sneakers and sandals and Parents' Day heels. There is dirt no one can get out of the cracks despite the mopping after each meal. All along her back a girl would be yellow if the years before her could disappear then make her new.

Pink is for the feeling of a puffy-eyed girl, in the infirmary with ice for her elbow and knee. She quietly opens the plastic bag and hits the ice on her face, making it spotty. It turns dark pink, then darker still. When she hits her arms, the skin on them turns blotchy like a rash she once had. She tries and tries, but the skin will not turn red.

White is the inside of the pool, underwater, where the girls open their eyes to play clapping games. Girls go under for just a second. Girls hold their breath, turn upside down, blow bubbles until they can't take it.

White is the color of leaving and coming up for air. It is the moment before the water breaks.

It is the color of the water in the night with the lights on.

It is the color of staying a girl, trapped in the only good sound.

Proof

She has the short hair of a girl whose mother has cut it. She wears the blouse of a girl whose mother picks out her clothes the night before.

"Who is this?" I ask, pointing to her picture on his yearbook page.

"She was slow," he says. "She used to come to the gas station where I worked."

The year of his yearbook is the year his father died.

"Did the retarded girl write in your yearbook?" I ask him.

"You mean slow," he says. "No."

His yearbook quote: *Summertime. Long days and nights with friends. Dance. Happiness is our goal, let's reach it!*

When you are slow it is fine to do things you can't do if you're not.

Below the retarded girl's picture is her quote:

We lost our best football game to Newport Harbor. The players were all on the field unconscious. I hugged the cheerleaders, Coach, and Trainer. We also lost the bell.

"Did you talk to her a lot?" I ask him.

"After my Dad died she walked over to the gas station and gave me a guitar."

"Wow," I say, "were you friends with her after that?"

"No," he says, "not really."

When his father died, he bought a used red sports car with the money he inherited and drove with the top down. He planned to be a businessman, a Republican, an acquirer of porcelain figurines his future wife would collect and put in glass cabinets.

When his father died, he was at home, waiting for him to get there and make dinner. His dad was always on time, so he watched the living room clock, the TV, and the window.

Meantime, his father was dying. He was running in his neighborhood down the streets he drove home on. He was running the same way he ran every evening after work, before he set the lawn chair on the front yard to watch the sun go down over the development across the way.

I lie in our bed with his yearbook. I touch my cat on her ear.

"Do you think there is something wrong with Chestnut's ears?" I ask.

Chestnut's ears have a small flap of fur-skin on the outside that seems to serve no purpose.

"No," he says and looks at me instead. "Your ears turn up at the lobes."

"Like my father's," I say.

But I am thinking of his mother. Soon she will get a lift in the neck where the skin hangs down into two drops like huge earlobes.

I look at his ears. They are made of fuzz and skin and cartilage. They are like noses that way.

When he sleeps, I push the little hair behind his ears. When he moves/snores/breathes, I am sure he is dreaming of black girls. Or at least the Asian mannequins we saw in the hairdresser's window with their submissive hair, falling straight to the floor, always obeying gravity.

"Do you still have the guitar?" I ask him.

"What guitar?" he says.

"The one the retarded girl gave you," I say.

"No. Her mother made her take it back," he says. "Slow."

"Why?" I say.

"Because she wasn't retarded."

"No, why did she take it back?"

"Oh," he says, "because it was her dead brother's and her mother wanted to keep it, I guess."

The year his father died, his mother took over. They had been divorced, and his mother had remarried and moved to France, while he had stayed in California with his father.

When his father died, his mother left her second husband, left France, and came to sleep again in the bed she once shared with his Dad. It was the bed his father once slept in alone.

His mother cooked, did his laundry, and made him rub lotion on her back. She said she couldn't reach, and she had left both men that used to do it for her.

When his father's best friend came over to tell him his father was dead, it wouldn't seep in.

"Is he okay?" he asked, since he had just seen his dad that morning, leaving for work. He had waved, smiled, and ducked his head in the car. His father had left before him.

And just the week before his father had had that talk with him again about his pot smoking, his laziness.

And wasn't it only a few days since his father had slammed his bedroom door so that he would wake up and help him with the trash?

"Your father's dead," his father's best friend said, straight from tennis and still in his tennis shorts.

His father's friend put his hand on his back and he looked at the hair on his legs. It was thick like his father's, but this man was not his father. When he closed his eyes the hand felt like his father's hand.

I imagine the girl:

She first smelled the best smell on her way home from the hospital, after she had gotten her adenoids out. She lay in the backseat, while her parents drove the station wagon.

She woke just as the boy was putting the gas in. She opened her eyes to a uniform-striped back leaning creased against the window. She reached her fingers up to touch the glass. When he turned around she saw his face upside down. He smiled but it looked like a frown like that.

She breathed in the smell of gas and he waved, all upside down. She was too tired to sit up. She smiled and waved back, but beneath her blanket where he couldn't see.

"So sad about his father," she heard her mother say as her father drove them farther away from the best smell, until she couldn't smell it anymore.

"Whose father?" she said, still lying down.

"Oh, honey, you're awake," her mother said, turning around to see her daughter.

"Whose father?" she said again.

"The gas station boy's, Sweetie. His daddy just died like Jakey did. Now try to sleep, Baby, we're almost home."

I imagine him:

When he looked in the back window of the car he saw her. Upside down, she looked pretty. He wasn't even sure who it was until he saw her parents.

"Fill her up," her father had said.

Her parents were normal, not slow.

Her brother hadn't been slow either. He had remembered her brother Jakey: older, on the school newspaper, a photographer or something. Kinda nerdy, he thought, smart.

Why is she lying under a blanket like that? He thought.

I wonder if she is sick too, he thought.

Poor family, he thought and waved to her.

His shift was almost done.

All of us eat quiche, fruit salad, and bagels. He and I eat tuna and lox, but his mother does not eat fish.

"Oh, fish," his mother says, tilting her mouth down more at the edges where it already turns that way. I believe she doesn't like fish because of the smell. The reason has something to do with her not liking women, but I have no proof.

All of us look at pictures of his dead father. The pictures are old.

His father is caught midair in a flip, on the sand of a beach we cannot see the water of.

His father with his pals on a road trip, posing with cigarettes against a dirty car.

"Your father never loved me," his mother says.

"Never?" I ask, since there are pictures, too, of them smiling. There are documents of her modeling career, two specially made wedding rings, a grown-up son.

"He just wanted children," his mother says.

All of us wish there was something to drink, but I know it is for the best that there is not. He knows how his mother gets when she is drinking, talking more and more about the dead.

"Did your mother know her?" I ask.

"Probably," he says. "I don't know."

We are in bed and he is falling asleep. He falls asleep quickly, his head on the mattress. His twitches, his stiffness, the parting and re-parting of his lips, have something to do with loving women, although I have no proof.

I imagine them:

After school he washed windshields, pumped gas, and got high behind the gas station garage. After his father died, he didn't have to listen for the wheels of his car and worry about getting caught anymore.

After his father died, he could quit his job if he wanted to, so he sat in the back and smoked cigarettes after smoking out. He even met his friends back there, sometimes.

The girl came with the guitar while he was smoking a cigarette. She walked out of the woods wearing a dress that looked too young for her. She carried the guitar over her shoulder like a rifle.

He watched her walk toward him and quickly stomped out his cigarette. He was glad he wasn't smoking dope. Although she probably wouldn't know the difference, he thought. With the light between the trees falling down on the grass back there, he thought she looked almost pretty.

"Hello," she said.

"Hi," he said.

She swung the guitar from around her and pulled the strap over her, and he thought she might start to play.

"Your dad died like Jakey did," she said.

"Yes," he said, "I'm sorry."

"Why?" she asked.

"I don't know," he said. "People die."

"Why are you sorry?" she asked.

"I don't know," he said. "I guess because they're dead."

He was trying to look at her eyes. The sun was shining brightly. It was a Sunday, and he put his hand on his forehead so he could see her better.

She walked a step closer to him and put her arms around him. In between them was the guitar, and as he put his arms back around her, the guitar bumped into his hipbone. She tried to lean her head where his shoulder would be, but there was too much space from the guitar, and her head fell to her neck in that space.

"This was Jakey's," she said, backing away.

She took the guitar off and handed it to him.

"I don't know how to play," he said.

"Learn," she said. "You can learn."

He held the guitar by the neck in one hand and she stepped toward him again. She leaned her head on his chest and he took his free arm and felt around to her back. He felt her bra strap as his arm went down her spine.

She was pressing close, hugging tightly around him. He put his face in her hair and felt himself getting hard.

"Thank you," he said.

He tried to think of the guitar but his hand went lower, pressing her into him. He held on tight to both the girl and the guitar.

As she swayed with him, he realized it was baby powder he was smelling, white clouds of it seeping from her hair.

*

While he sleeps I watch him and look through his yearbook. I try to pick out the popular girls and the boys I would have liked if I had gone to his high school.

He is twitching again, and I nudge him. He opens his eyes in slits.

"What?" he says.

"Nothing," I say.

"Is something wrong?" he asks.

I sigh and close the book. Our cat jumps on our bed. I bring his arms around me and face away from him.

I want to turn off the light, but I also want to talk.

"So, what happened with the girl?"

"What?" he asks, half sleeping.

When I turn around his eyes are closed. I watch the pupils below his lids move from side to side. I want to put my fingers there to stop him from dreaming.

I imagine myself a girl another girl will hold pictures of.

"Who is this?" she'll say to my boyfriend who is trying to sleep beside her.

She will hold a photo of my face that I had taken of myself, holding the camera at arm's length.

She will find another photo where my hair is still long, and another where I had cut it off.

She will fingerprint a photo where I sit with my mother and smile while my mother eats cereal in the background.

"Her?" he'll say.

Jet Man

Steve told Alice about Jack Conlon, a guy who had been in his early twenties the summer Steve was just eleven. Jack Conlon was the janitor at their school for July and August. Steve and his next-door neighbor, Benji, began talking to him while they skateboarded on the playground and Jack smoked and watched outside.

Jack told Steve and Benji that he had a girlfriend named Darla, but by the end of the summer the two boys still hadn't seen her. He told them she had big tits and wore bodysuits that she left unbuckled in the crotch for "easy access."

After he showed them the janitor closet and took them on a tour of the dark school basement, Jack told them he would pay each boy a dollar an hour if they helped him work. Steve didn't understand why things had to be so clean in the summers but that was Jack's job for now. He had the boys wash windows, pick gum off of the bottom of the desks, and sometimes just keep him company. After the summer, Jack said he was going to Colorado. He had other things going, he told them. He was the second-best badminton player in the country, but since badminton was not a professional sport, he couldn't make money that way. Instead he got free beers for winning, he said, and Darla went to every match and always called his name.

Jack Conlon asked Steve and Benji to sleep over at his apartment, even though he was older. They all slept together, side by side in Jack's water bed. It was the most comfortable bed and the boys were still small. Jack slept in the middle, moving the water beneath him while he turned toward Steve. He kept his hands on the side of his cheek, making a pillow, or halfway praying, as if he were saying his prayers all night long.

"So then what happened?" Alice asked Steve after he finished telling her. They were lying in bed in their bedroom, both looking at the ceiling. Alice watched the fan that had come with the house go around and around and around.

"Nothing," Steve said.

"Then why are you telling me?" she asked.

It was typical that he would say something like this, something so obviously strange, and then act like nothing was wrong with it. It was as if he wanted her to have a reaction so that he wouldn't have to. Alice had the feelings for what Steve had thought all along.

"Well, don't you think, looking back, that it was strange for a twenty-something man to have a sleepover with two little boys? In his water bed? Are you sure nothing happened?"

Steve took her in his arms and squeezed her tightly. Alice noticed that when he felt uncomfortable, or when he wanted her to see things his way, his grip on her shoulder got tighter; his hand in her hair pulled her scalp.

"Baby," Alice said, "give me some room."

When Steve spoke of his childhood, overcast with his sunny avoidance of things, his voice had the happiness of a ten-year-old. Alice loved to hear about his early life—it was so different from her own—but sometimes it felt like Steve could not look back on his youth with any reflection.

Steve would always start his stories with some boy with a name like Chad Peters or Tucker Nielsen; a boy who now lived somewhere entirely different, now a man with children, probably far from his Arizona upbringing, just like they were, in their rural Vermont home.

Alice loved Steve's stories, even if he couldn't see them the way she did. His whole childhood was bright in her mind, and she imagined it in the saturated colors of old film.

"Ugh," Steve said, "tomorrow is Monday . . . "

It was the present, when Steve spoke about their life as it was, that always brought Alice back to her thoughts about how she might rearrange the pictures on the wall. She did not want to hear about his day. She wanted to hear what he remembered.

Drum up something, she often thought. *Drum up something new.*

Anything, she thought, *so that I will love you.*

Think back to the time when your hair was as yellowy-white as the room we have painted, when your thighs were not tight the way they are now, but naturally nice, like your dad's. Was there something, some story you forgot to tell me? she wondered.

She loved the boy he had once been. She had not known him then, but there were traces of his child self all over him as a man. He looked like a baby dinosaur just hatched from his egg in the morning; his eyebrows stayed light even though his hair was dark now; he was pigeon-toed in only one foot. These things saved him every day.

Steve and Alice lived in a small house set back from a big road. It was a house that used to be the servants' quarters for the larger house. The larger house was still owned by the Hardley's, a family that once had servants. Now the big house was run-down, and the Hardley's only came to stay in it during the summer.

During the rest of the year, Steve and Alice could live cheaply if they mowed the lawn and looked out for the property. They had the keys to the big house and once a month they used them. Once a month they cooked a dinner at their own house and put on nice clothes. Then they carried the dinner, covered in tin foil and hot in their hands, like caterers, to the big house.

They walked through the large front hall, Steve behind Alice, because Steve was always a little scared and lit candles that they brought, to the large oak-paneled dining room. Alice would wear either her black dress with the pink flowers that she bought on sale or her teak sarong. Steve liked the sarong, Alice knew, because the last time she wore it he began kissing her before they even started eating and ended up on the floor while their dinner got cold.

Steve was often tired when he got home. During the day he was the head editor at the local newspaper for a town two towns over. He had a secretary he hated but was afraid to fire, not because he was worried that he wouldn't be able to find someone else, but because she was mean and fat. Alice thought he just liked to complain about her: she dressed with bunched-up socks and sneakers over panty hose; she ignored him when he asked her to close the door on her way out. He liked to tell Alice while he sat naked, eating his dinner, about the rashes the secretary would get on her face, and the way she scratched them, flaking skin on his letters.

Sometimes when Steve was at work, Alice would go inside the big house and stand in the sun spots on the Hardley's bedroom floor. All the furniture in the house was covered in sheets, and in the summer, before the Hardley's came home, it was Alice's job to take the sheets off. The Hardley's never once asked Alice and Steve over when they were there; they were old and not very friendly.

On regular nights, after dinner, Alice and Steve would sit on their couch naked and watch television. They did not have certain shows they watched, and they did not have cable. Instead they flicked from one channel to the other, usually with Alice in control of the remote, while touching each other's legs with their toes. Often, Alice made the mistake of trying to tell Steve about her day while they were flipping channels. It did not seem to matter what they were watching—a local commercial for sofa beds featuring the owner of the store's three-year-old jumping on a mattress, or even a rerun of a show they had seen before—Steve would be too distracted to hear her. So, as Alice began to tell him about how Joanna, the girl she babysat for, had built a psychiatrist's couch for her dolls and had made a rug with white cloth that she colored with small triangles to imitate the look of Freud's woven rugs, she knew that she was only talking so she could pretend they were having a conversation.

Alice and Steve did not have children, but Alice loved small kids and was a nanny for ten-year-old Joanna during the day. Joanna was skinny but beautiful with long black hair she always wore down. She named her Barbies after the ancient Greeks. She had two Aphrodites, and one Ken named Zeus. She had an Achilles and an Iphegenia, and a doll she kept in her drawer with a bandage around her leg, tied up with a green piece of string.

Joanna's mother, Diane, worked on their property in the small, experimental theater she had started, inside an old barn. The theater was sparse, with wood-plank bleachers for seats. The plays were written with a specific technique in which the actors got together and then wrote a script from their own experiences and relationships during the time they were writing it. People would come to the small barn from far away—even other countries—just to play make-believe.

It was hard to believe that Diane was Joanna's mother, the way she flung herself on the experimental stage, making it creak. Joanna was such a poised girl, already ready for the needs of a million doll babies that called her name so only she could hear them. Her mother was oblivious, coming home from the theater with bruises on her legs and arms, the new ones purple, the old a fading brick into her skin.

Sometimes Joanna, asleep with Cleopatra in her arms, and Alice took walks to the barn to watch practices. Joanna told Alice that her mother's sister, her Aunt Vel, did not believe in going into the arts as a profession. Aunt Vel gave Diane money, Joanna said. She told her how she planned to be like her aunt when she grew up.

They took walks through the fields in the afternoons, and Alice told Joanna stories. Joanna liked to hear how she had met Steve. She wanted to hear about it again and again, so each day Alice would make up a new story about their meeting.

In Joanna's favorite story (she told her while she brushed her hair and Joanna brushed the dolls'), Alice and Steve had met on a train. They were in a small sleeping-car room going from Spain to Italy. There were six beds in the room and four were filled with old men, all brothers. When they had turned out the lights at night, all four of the men began to snore. There was an open window so the summer air blew in on Alice's face.

Alice told Joanna how she had lain awake on the highest bunk bed above two of the brothers who slept in matching brown pants. Her face was an inch from the red painted ceiling. When she turned on her side her ear scraped the wall. She held onto the side of the thin bed so not to fall off, listening to the train that made a song beneath her.

"Were you hot?" Joanna asked. Joanna was often sweating. Alice wondered if there was something wrong with her, and if her father had been like that too. Alice had never met Joanna's father—she had only seen the one picture that Joanna kept of him in her jewelry box. He wore a white suit and had a mustache. His eyes were squinting against the sun in a field; he was standing alone.

"Not too bad. It felt kind of cozy," Alice said. She worried about scaring Joanna, telling her something that would show up in her dreams. She wanted Joanna to remember her when she was older and to ask Diane about her when she no longer needed a babysitter.

Alice went on, telling Joanna about how she woke up in the middle of the night and tried to sit up, but bumped her forehead. She could see that someone had moved into the bed across from her—he had a flashlight and was reading a book with a butterfly on the cover.

"Hello," the man said, "I'm Steve. Do you speak English?"

Alice nodded, hitting her head two more times.

The men below them snored as Alice and Steve faced each other all night, whispering at first and then laughing, using only one hand to talk because the other was crushed beneath their sides.

"What did he say?" Joanna asks.

"He said that he could see the shine of my hair in the light from his flashlight, and that my curls looked like little question marks all over my head. He said that he was traveling— that he had just been to a castle where a king had once ordered a feast so big that he had to throw up after he ate."

"Eeeewww!" Joanna said. Sometimes Alice forgot she was talking to a child. She loved to watch Joanna's face take each story in. It was a child's face, but her expressions were so intense that it made Alice want to make her stories more and more romantic.

The sad truth was that Alice and Steve had met while working at a small newspaper in the city. She was an assistant in the photography department, trying to help her boss match pictures with headlines and continually getting them wrong. Steve was an editor, and they had met at a retirement party for someone neither of them knew. They had each thought, for some reason, that they were supposed to bring the cake; they each picked the same cake—a small chocolate one with pink words. Steve's said, "GOOD LUCK"; Alice's said, "CHEERS TO 20 YEARS."

Alice had gotten drunk on white wine, and Steve had asked her out to dinner. She remembered how the wine had made her feel, and how Steve had seemed like someone who was trustworthy and smart. He took off his tie, and Alice noticed how his chest hair was shaved or cut into a collar at his collar bone.

"Can we go for Mexican?" Alice had asked, and Steve had told her, leaning his arm across her to the wall, that they could go anywhere she wanted.

"Anywhere?" Alice asked.

"Well, not anywhere . . . " Steve told her, looking away from her at the rest of the conference room, where suddenly everyone seemed to be getting their coats on.

The next night they went out for Mexican. Alice had eaten so many chips that she wasn't even hungry when her dinner came. She also drank strawberry margaritas, sweet and frozen, with salt on the sides of the glasses. She wasn't sure how to get the salt off without licking the rim and then drinking, but after a few she forgot to lick and sipped her margarita quickly with her straw.

Steve told her stories about his strange landlord and moving to the city from Arizona. He had a strange inflection; it was hard to tell sometimes if he was kidding or not. She laughed anyway. It was funny.

That night he walked her back to her apartment that she shared with her roommate. The roommate was asleep, so they had sex in the den on the couch that Alice had had sex on before. They left the TV on, since they had gone to her apartment on the premise that they would watch a video.

The sex was quick, and Steve was quiet. Alice knew she surprised him when she talked dirty, trying to get him to moan.

"Let me hear you," she had said.

They had been together ever since.

There was one room in Diane and Joanna's house that Alice was not supposed to go in. It was an office with a low door frame you had to duck beneath to get into.

Diane had put purple stained glass on the windows in the room. She had pillows with gold brocade and candles covered in dust. Alice knew Diane brought her boyfriend there sometimes. Or her lover, Alice wasn't sure. He was the set man for Diane's plays. She saw him in the theater or walking around the fields in the distance, up on the slope of the theater's property. He had long blond hair and a long torso; he wore his pants low so that his short legs looked shorter, his rib cage longer. Alice did not like his long hair, but she could see what Diane saw in him sometimes. He sat on the porch of the theater, smoking cigarettes and looking at the sky.

Some nights, after Joanna went to bed and the performance was still going, Alice sat in Diane's special room. From where she sat on the pillows, looking out into the hall, the room felt smothering and small.

The newest play had something to do with horses. Alice lay on the pillows in the room and listened for the last applause from the audience. She waited a while, then walked across the driveway to the theater and stood in the side doorway. The set man was shirtless, taking down blue cellophane from the lights. The blue shadows looked like puddles on his back.

He seemed to be hammering one nail for a long time. Alice had forgotten about Diane. She watched him, moving her hand across one of the wood boards on the doorframe until a splinter pierced her skin.

"Ow!" Alice said, looking up at the man as soon as she said it. Joanna had told her that before he was the set man there was a lesbian who had the job who left to have a baby.

Alice could feel herself blush. The set man was looking straight at her, and Alice stepped from behind the boards into his blue light.

"You okay?" he asked. He walked down the ladder and pulled his pants up from the back.

"Yes. Sorry. I'm just looking for Diane."

"You're the babysitter," he said, walking over toward her with his arm outstretched. She noticed he was bow-legged, something that had always repulsed Alice; it made her think of an arthritic cat she had had as a child.

"I'm Gabriel," he said. He shook her hand. His palm was dry. She wondered if it was dry from the wood. She imagined that at night he brought sawdust with him under the covers where he rubbed his feet together until it turned into a fine powder, his skin coated with it in the morning.

Gabriel smiled and his upper lip disappeared. He had thick, white teeth.

"I'm Alice," she said. "I just wanted to pick up my check."

"Diane went out with the cast for a bit, I think. Do you want a beer?" he asked, walking over to the theater fridge that was next to the plank that was the theater's first row.

"Sure," said Alice.

It was like Diane to be late. Diane was supposed to go up to the house right after Alice left, as soon as she paid her, so that Joanna would not be alone. Alice worried about Joanna being burned in a fire when she was not there. Sometimes, when Alice had to leave before Diane came home from shopping, she worried that Diane would forget, wandering in the fruit aisle and debating between peaches and nectarines, melons, and cantaloupe. She could get lost there, Alice thought. Sometimes it seemed impossible that Joanna had survived so long without Alice.

Alice sat down in the front row and Gabriel handed her a cold beer. He opened his own and sipped quickly, then wiped his mouth with his hand.

"How's babysitting going?" he asked.

Alice wondered if he thought she was a teenager. She had often been mistaken for one. She still had on the pink barrettes Joanna had put in her hair while they were playing "hairdresser."

Alice twirled her wedding ring with her other hand.

"Joanna is a great girl," she said, trying to sound like an adult who studied Joanna all day instead of a woman who got on her hands and knees each afternoon in order to put all Joanna's dolls in her dollhouse down for a nap. From the small dollhouse windows, Alice knew she looked big, covering the dolls with potholder covers, like she was trying to climb inside.

"Yes, she seems to be. Very imaginative."

Alice wondered when Joanna and Gabriel might have met. She wondered if he slept over and stayed for breakfast the next morning. Joanna had never mentioned him, and Alice wondered if Diane actually had enough mothering skills to know that it would be best if Joanna did not see every man her mother slept with.

"Yes, she is," Alice said, proudly. She liked to think that she had something to do with how great Joanna was, even though she knew that Joanna had been the way she was since she was born. She wondered how much Diane had to do with it. Alice felt jealous knowing that Diane probably had a lot to do with it.

"I thought Diane was going to go home after the show," Alice said.

She did not have anywhere important to be—Steve would be asleep when she got home—but Alice worried about being in this blue light, alone with Diane's man. Suddenly she could hear the refrigerator buzzing, the barn making noises, the wind through the wood.

"I think she'll be back soon," Gabriel said. He did not sound annoyed. He turned his head sideways, looking at Alice, and took another big sip of the beer.

"I'm sure I can front you the money if you are in a rush," he started to straighten one of his legs and reached in his jean pocket.

"Oh no, no, no," Alice said, "that's okay."

"All right," he said, shrugging. "Well, you're welcome to wait here. I'm just starting to make the set for the next play. It's hard to know what she wants, though. She keeps changing her mind."

"Diane?" Alice asked.

"Yeah," Gabriel was looking at the boards in the middle of the stage he had been nailing together, "I've been making plans and redoing them for the past month. Every time I'm almost finished she tells me it's wrong. At my old job—"

"Where did you used to work?" Alice was suddenly very curious, but she wasn't sure why.

"I've never been a set builder before. Actually, I was a plumber two towns over. But I saw the job in the paper, and my ex-wife and I were living too close to each other, so I decided to take it."

Alice was disappointed. She realized that she had been imagining him as some kind of professional who would be able to make beautiful sets that moved and transformed and looked like Joanna's drawings. Sadly, he only worked with water that came through metal pipes for toilets and sinks and washing machines.

"Oh," Alice said, "I thought you were involved with the theater."

"No, no," he said, "I don't know shit about this stuff."

Alice thought he might be lying. How could he be a plumber?

Alice heard the sound of the side door opening, and they both turned to see Joanna's long nightgowned shadow spread across the floor from the floodlights outside.

"Why did you leave me alone?" she yelled. Alice could see she was crying.

"Oh, I'm sorry, honey," Alice said, running up to hug her.

Joanna ran past her, and onto the stage where she hugged Gabriel's legs.

"Joanna, I just thought your mom was going to be home soon," Alice said, getting down on her knees so that she could pull her off of Gabriel.

"Stop it!" Joanna yelled.

"Honey," she said.

"I want my mommy," she yelled.

"Your mommy will be home soon," Gabriel said.

"I'm sorry," Alice said.

"Where is she?" Joanna yelled.

"Should I take her back to bed?" Alice asked Gabriel.

"I don't want to go back to bed," Joanna answered.

"Sit here with us," Gabriel said.

"I want to go home," Joanna said.

Gabriel took Joanna's face and gently lifted it up to look at him.

"She's sleepwalking," he whispered. "Look at her eyes."

Alice walked over quietly, onto the stage. Joanna's beautiful eyes were halfway open and unfocused.

Alice wished Gabriel would scoop her up in his arms the way he did to Joanna, whose eyes had closed into sleep again. She wanted to be Joanna when she followed Gabriel up to her bedroom where he held her and then stepped back so Alice could tuck her in. She put Cleopatra next to her so Joanna would wake up and know where she was.

Alice followed Gabriel back down the stairs, peeking into the forbidden room. She wanted to go back to the stage where she could star in a play on the thick wood of Gabriel's planks. She would sing about horses and act on her knees. She would do whatever she needed to do. Anything. As long as she could stay in his blue light; as long as she didn't have to go home.

Tag Sale

Robin parked on the grass outside the old yellow house and waited while her mother flipped down the mirror to put her lipstick on. It was morning: the first tag sale of the day. They had planned to come early, but already they had been beaten by a woman with a baby asleep in one of those front-facing baby holders, and a couple with matching hiking boots. Robin and her mother walked onto the lawn to see what was for sale.

While her mother went straight toward a bed frame, Robin focused on a clear glass paperweight with a purple flower frozen inside. It was their first summer in the area and for the past few weekends Robin had gone with her mother to look for furniture to fill their new New England summer home. They were supposed to be looking for large things like bureaus and tables.

Robin put the paperweight up to her eye to see if she could see through it.

"Over here are the good things," she heard a man with an accent say. She turned around and saw a tall, thin man gesturing and talking to her mother. He had gray hair and the kind of sunglasses that you could see yourself in.

German? Robin wondered, *Israeli?*

Robin's mother motioned for her to come over so she put the paperweight down and followed them onto the porch.

"I have many nice things," the man said, pulling up his sunglasses. He looked about her mother's age. His face was filled with gray stubble and around his blue eyes there were wrinkles. He had a bump on his nose.

Jew? Robin wondered.

"Beautiful things," Robin's mother said, swiping her red polished fingernails across a dusty coffee table.

"This is a featherbed made in Europe," the man said in his accent. He leaned over and she could see the skin on his thin stomach. He pointed to a thick pink comforter half folded on a chest of drawers.

"Beautiful," Robin said.

There was a breeze and Robin touched the comforter. It plumped back in the space her hand left when she raised her palm from it, and she imagined the comforter on her bed. She wondered if it was okay to sleep on a featherbed that someone else had owned, or if it was like shoes: something you should always get new. Maybe featherbeds were for sleeping on the floor. She was sure her mother would know.

"How much for me?" Robin's mother asked the foreign man. She looked at Robin who had been imagining the featherbed on the floor in her own new room.

"For you?" the man said. He laughed.

He put his sunglasses back on and Robin couldn't tell where he was looking until he put his hand out.

"I'm Jacob," the man said, shaking her mother's hand.

German, Robin thought.

Robin and her mother introduced themselves, and her mother explained how they had just bought the old house on the hill to use as a summer house. She explained how they were from the city, how Robin was staying for the summer but she and her husband would only be up on weekends.

He nodded.

"Well, I'll be moving soon," he said, "so I need to sell my things. Would you like to come inside and see more of my pieces?"

The mother with the baby had already gone. As Robin closed the screen door behind her she watched the woman on the lawn holding the glass paperweight with the purple flower frozen inside, turning it back and forth in her hands.

When her eyes adjusted to the inside of Jacob's house she saw half-packed boxes he lined up from the foyer to the next room. There were also things on the floor he hadn't packed yet, as if he were still deciding whether he really wanted to leave.

Jacob stood in the hall with his arms crossed. He looked old in a strange way. He had wrinkles, but there was something good-looking about him too. Maybe it was his eyes.

"Beautiful floors," Robin's mother said, looking down.

Jacob put his hands together and Robin looked at his long bony fingers. His fingernails were dirty and she wondered whether that was from packing or they were always that way.

"Do you collect?" he asked. "Are you into Deco?"

He turned before they could answer and they followed him. He stopped in his kitchen where the cabinets were wood, but there was an old refrigerator in a bad green color, and dirty pots and pans on the nice granite counters.

Robin's mother began to tell him again about their house.

"I like things that I can use," Jacob interrupted, pointing to a napkin holder on the table. There were three napkins in it and on the outside were two girls carved into the metal, facing each other.

"Deco," Jacob said, looking at Robin staring at it.

His accent made Robin think he was lying.

Robin's mother picked up the holder.

"Noses like ours," Robin's mother said, putting one finger onto Robin's forehead and her nose.

The two girls on the napkin holder faced each other. They were twins: sisters with noses like the statue of David. They were Greeks or Jews.

"If I can use things," Jacob said, "then I keep them."

Robin and her mother did not collect. Robin's mother's sister—Robin's aunt—collected anything that had a poodle on it. She had poodles made of Legos, looking like pencil sharpeners or ashtrays; anything that could take a shape could become a poodle.

Robin turned to look out the front window behind her. On the window sill was a picture of Jacob with his arm around a woman, kissing her hair in that father way, on the side of her forehead. The photograph was large in a cheap thin frame. Robin wondered when he would pack it.

"My wife was Jewish," Jacob said, pointing to the photograph she had been looking at on the window.

"Really," Robin's mother said. Robin nodded and wondered how long his wife had been dead. She wondered if what he was telling them was strange, since they had not said anything about being Jewish. Or maybe he was trying to let them know that he wasn't Jewish himself. Robin's family was sure they were one of the only Jewish families around; their new town consisted of one road with three churches and a gas station.

"Excuse my mess," Jacob said, quickly turning before she could ask more questions. Robin and her mother followed him.

The living room was empty except for a fireplace. There were dents in the carpet where a sofa must have been. The only other thing in the room was a painting of his wife on the mantle. Here she was in color, younger, her face tilted in a strange way. She had hair like Robin's—black and long.

"Excuse my mess," he said again, reaching into a closet on the other side of the room. He began to take out different plates wrapped in cloth. He unwrapped each one gently and handed them one at a time to her mother.

"All hand painted," he said.

Robin leaned over to see the plates, all white with tiny black silhouettes of men and women standing next to each other on the edges. The same woman's shape stood next to the same man's shape all around the plate. The men wore hats; the women had high heels.

"Beautiful," Robin said, and Jacob nodded.

In the car Robin looked out the window while her mother drove. The houses were far apart here, set back, with lots of land. She wondered how people met each other out here. She wondered why people lived out here in the first place. She wondered about the little worlds going on in each house, and about Jacob, with all his things.

"We should try to fix him up with someone," her mother said as they turned onto the town's main road.

"He seems like he's still grieving, though," her mother said. Since her mother's father had died last winter, her mother was always talking about grief.

"Maybe he's always like that," Robin said.

In the photograph of Jacob and his wife he looked younger; it didn't seem like a woman had been in the house for a long time.

"I think he's German, don't you?" her mother asked, turning up their gravel-covered driveway.

"Maybe," Robin said.

The next day, after her parents had left for the city, Robin got in her car and drove to Jacob's road.

The tag sale signs were gone, and she wondered if Jacob had taken them down. He didn't seem like someone who did that kind of thing. She couldn't imagine him putting the signs up either. She imagined him at home, reading, smoking cigarettes, looking at pictures of his dead wife while he was still in his bathrobe.

Robin pulled into the driveway. On the porch and on the lawn were still a few unsold desks and chairs. It looked creepy with all that furniture outside now that the sale was over.

"Hello," she said, opening the door just a crack after she had knocked and heard nothing.

She stepped into the front hall and Jacob came slowly out of the living room. He wore a T-shirt and corduroys: two different, clashing, shades of brown. His glasses were pushed up on his head, like other people wore sunglasses.

"Hello," he said, calmly, as if he was expecting her.

She looked past him to the painting of his wife.

"I came to see if you were still selling the featherbed?" Robin asked.

"The featherbed," he said, walking into the kitchen. "I've just been packing things."

Robin followed him, "Where are you moving to?"

"Not far. Just a few miles down the road. I just don't want to be in this house anymore," he said.

Jacob motioned for her to sit in a chair at the kitchen table while he went over to the stove. She wondered if he was moving closer to their house.

"Would you like tea?" Jacob asked.

"Sure," Robin said. She sat and watched him from behind as he turned on the burner. His pants were held up by a thin black belt and she looked at his white elbows and the bumps of his shoulders and the places in his pants where his corduroys were faded.

Jacob brought the napkin holder with the two girls to the table from the shelf and took a napkin out for each of them.

"How are you liking it here?" he asked, sitting across from her.

She told him she planned to swim at the lake and read a lot this summer. She had to get a job but there were no jobs so far that she qualified for. There were so many books she wanted to read, she said, and there was not much else to do.

"Yes," Jacob said. "It is very peaceful here."

She got up from the table to look out the back window above the sink. His backyard was unmowed and ended in a line of trees. She turned and watched as Jacob tipped his head back, gulping the tea. Then he slammed the teacup down on the table as if he had just taken a shot.

"Would you like to take a drive?" Jacob said suddenly, and smiled, showing crooked teeth for the first time.

Robin chauffeured Jacob. She opened up the sunroof and all four windows and drove fast once they got onto the paved road.

With the windows down she could only hear the air. It reminded her of being little on the beach, lying on the sand with her eyes closed and hearing the lispy whisper of her mother's voice.

She looked over at Jacob whose eyes were closed, head tilted back. His grayish hair was flapping like dog ears.

He opened his eyes.

"What did you say?" Jacob yelled.

"I didn't say anything," Robin yelled back into the wind, after looking into his eyes for just a second, and then turning away, back to the road.

Up ahead was a tower with three stories of stairs leading up to a small platform at the top. A sign with green letters said, "CLIMB AND SEE THREE STATES!"

Robin had passed the tower of platforms and stairs the week before and wondered if the structure was sound. It looked like scaffolding, like it was waiting to be finished, like it was missing its walls.

Robin slowed down.

"Want to go there?" she asked.

He looked up and nodded so she turned into the driveway of the small tourist shop.

"Have you done this before?" Robin asked as she held the door of the shop behind her.

"No," he said. "Never."

She wondered if he had a daughter. She must look like his daughter, she thought, to the woman behind the counter who smiled at them when they came in. She imagined herself having a sleepover at his house with his daughter and sleeping on the pink featherbed together while they listened to the sound of Jacob, late at night, making another cup of tea.

Inside the store were small Indian dolls, Beanie Babies, scented candles, and homemade pins that said, "I saw three states . . . and survived!"

Jacob was standing with his hands in his pockets, then took out his wallet from his back pocket and paid for them.

Robin went through the door that said, "This way . . . " and Jacob followed her.

His head hit the ceiling, and suddenly she was embarrassed for him. Surrounded by small things he did not own, he looked like someone who might steal them.

Jacob rubbed his head and stepped into the sun behind her.

"Up here," she said, pointing to the first set of steps. From the bottom, it looked like a long way to the top. It occurred to Robin she did not know what three states she was going to see and whether the state they were in was part of the deal or not.

Robin went up the first set of steps and then looked down from the top of the first platform. Jacob was still standing on the black tar of the ground.

"Come on," she said to him as he looked up at her, his hand shielding his eyes from the sun.

"I'm coming," he said. She watched as he climbed the stairs, slowly, holding onto the railing. She sat down on the platform, her feet on the last step, and looked out onto the land. She imagined that once she was at the top platform the states would have lines separating them like on a map, and they would differentiate themselves by turning different pastel colors. Their names would be spelled out in relief.

"Aren't we supposed to climb more?" Jacob asked. He was now on the step where Robin sat, looking down at her. Then he sat down.

Robin saw a hole in his corduroys, on his upper thigh, that she could see his pale skin and black wiry hair peeking out of. He took out a crumpled soft pack of cigarettes from his pocket.

"Want one?" he asked. He smoked cigarettes just like she had imagined.

Jacob lit her cigarette and stared at Robin while she took a drag. She looked back at him and then out at the trees.

"What is your story, Robin?" he asked, blowing his smoke in her face. He felt too close, and his smoke bothered her even though she was smoking too. Suddenly his leg was touching hers.

Robin looked back at him and laughed, trying to think what he thought her story was, trying to inch herself away from him so they weren't touching anymore. She was not sure she wanted to tell him.

She looked down, trying to think of what to say. She wondered if this all had been a mistake. Did he even still have the featherbed? He had never told her, and now they were past all that, sitting together on a platform, no one else around.

"Oh, Robin," he said and his accent annoyed her. The tone of his voice made him sound like he knew what she was thinking. He patted her bare knee with his hand, "You have a story."

"What do you want to know?" Robin asked.

Jacob smiled and did not say anything. Robin flicked her cigarette away. She stood up and pulled her shorts down on her hips.

"Let's keep going," she said.

Jacob followed her up to the second platform where she sat again and he stood. She played with her shoelaces and suddenly felt his hands on her shoulders.

"Robin," he said, and she wished he wouldn't say her name.

"What?" she asked.

"There are more steps," he said, taking his hands away.

Robin followed Jacob up the third set of steps. He took the steps two at a time, his shadow shading her. Suddenly he seemed anxious to get to the top.

She wanted to be on the ground again, in the state she had been in when she had gone to Jacob's house to buy a featherbed. Robin held onto the banister and looked down. She had heard once that the only people who were afraid of heights were the ones who were tempted to jump. Robin wondered if she was tempted but she couldn't tell.

She took a breath and followed Jacob until they got to the top. Jacob stood leaning against the railing. He leaned forward into the empty sky.

"I've got so much more to clean up," he said, "I'm dreading it."

Robin stood on the platform, far from the edge. She looked out at the land.

"Yeah, that stinks," she said.

"I have so many things," he said, "that I don't use."

Robin shook her head and tried to see if she could find her new house.

"Why don't you just bury them?" she said and laughed, then stopped, remembering. "I mean . . . " she said, turning to look the other way.

"Hey," Jacob said.

Robin turned back to see him smiling again. His front teeth were brown, probably because the water from wherever he was from had no fluoride.

"Come here, Robin," Jacob said. She turned and saw Jacob's fingers wiggling toward her, waiting. She wondered how his Jewish wife had loved him, if they had been as young as she was when she fell for him, and if their love was beautiful when she was alive, or only seemed that way now that she was gone.

Robin stepped closer, but not close enough. The wind blew. She thought about the featherbed on someone else's bed somewhere, already taking the shape of a new mattress, taking the shape of another girl. Perhaps a smarter girl, who had known to snatch the featherbed up as soon as she saw it. Maybe a girl who got it first, before her mother staked her claim.

There was no real reason she had not bought the featherbed yesterday. Or the paperweight she had loved. She should have had them now, instead of being at the top of a platform with a man who was probably a German.

"Do you still have the featherbed?" she asked, standing still.

Jacob stopped wiggling his fingers.

"Maybe," he said, smiling like it was funny.

Robin turned to take the first step down. She wanted to drive back and rummage through his boxes. It felt like he had stolen all her things, all the things that should fill her house. She wanted to drive back and load up the car with all his boxes and leave him with his painting, his house, his pictures, and his napkin holder.

"I think we should go," she said.

"First come here, Robin," he said, "please."

She looked at his face; his blue eyes were bright, almost crazy looking. When he said her name it made her sad.

Robin walked toward him, as he held onto the railing again. There was a space there for her, between his hands and arms and the railing. She could fit there, she saw.

She looked out where he was looking now. There was land that was green, some brown, two tiny towns that she could see clearly, two graveyards. There were mountains far off, and trees that covered her view of houses. There were all the signs of life: cars moving, smoke coming from chimneys, but she was too high up to see it.

Up on the small platform, there was space enough for both of them; there was space she could fit herself into and there was space where she could fit someone else inside her arms.

There was nothing else for them to hold at the top.

She felt herself moving toward him. She let him surround her with his arms. Robin let him hold her, just like that, wondering if she was scared, and if he would stop her from falling.

The Neutered Bulldog

When my teacher began her affair, she told me about it on the rug where it had happened. We were in the second-floor study of her house—above her husband's office—where she had first kissed Brian Wojowsky.

The floor was hard with only a thin rug on top of it. She had a couch but they hadn't used it, and while she told me, neither did we. I sat on the wood part, facing her book-shelves, while she leaned against the wall and smoked one of my cigarettes. It was during lunch hour, and soon we would both have to be back at school.

"Brian is in my gym class and my math class next period," I told her. I took the cigarette from her thin freckled fingers and blew smoke into the dusty light.

"Really?" she said. She took the cigarette back and stubbed it out in the ceramic ashtray she hid from her husband, Ed. "I didn't know that."

I got up and pulled my jeans down on my waist. If I was late for math I could get a detention, and my teacher had already written me a bunch of notes. She couldn't write too many more. Boys were already saying things.

"What does Brian wear in gym class?" she asked, getting up and looking in the mirror that was next to her computer. She ran her fingers around the rim of her lips.

I had never thought about Brian in gym class before. He was not someone I noticed. He was small, for one, and not attractive in the way I liked boys I couldn't have. I saved my fantasies for the best. Brian was thin and quiet and didn't play sports.

"I don't know," I laughed, walking down the stairs to the living room where she had lined the windows with rocks and shells and beach glass she had found. "Shorts and a T-shirt, probably."

My teacher followed me and we walked out the door together.

"See you tomorrow—third period," she said, getting into her car. "I'll be busy tonight," she said, and winked.

On the first day of school, in the beginning of fall, I called my teacher Mrs. Holly. She wasn't my teacher then the way that she is now. On the first day of school she wore glasses and her hair pulled back. She wore a pleated skirt that was too long to show her perfect calves that tapered to her knee in exactly the right place.

The desks were already in a circle when we got to class so we all sat around and tried not to look at one another. Mrs. Holly was a new teacher, and no one told her we weren't used to sitting that way.

"I'd like to go around the room and have everyone tell a little bit about themselves," she had said. She pointed at me, "Starting with you."

"Moldy," one of the boys whispered loud enough so everyone could hear. I rolled my eyes and ignored him.

I had been nicknamed "Moldy" because my last name is Gold and it rhymed. Sometimes they called me Moldy Matzoh because I am Jewish.

I had been drawing in my notebook, making circles inside of circles. I did not want to go first.

"Um . . . " I said. "My name is Sarah. I'm sixteen years old. I don't play any sports."

"Okay," Mrs. Holly said, smiling. "Tell us a dream."

"A nighttime dream?" I asked. My dreams were filled with colors and boys and people without any genitals rubbing up against each other.

"No, a daytime dream," Alec Ryerson said and there were laughs around the circle.

"I pass," I said, that first day.

I handed in my first poem to Mrs. Holly after our second class. The poem, "P is for Prozac," was about a girl who commits suicide. It did not rhyme. When I read it in class, Mrs. Holly smiled and asked me to stay afterward. She told me that I was a poet, like her.

After class, we sat at the desks, next to each other.

"You remind me of me," she said.

I blushed because she was beautiful. She was tall with reddish hair and I was tall but did not look like her. I looked at the width of her freckled wrist and compared it to my own.

"I would love for you to come over some time," she said. "It's important for poets to stick together."

I nodded at my teacher and looked away from her eyes.

"I'm a person too, you know," she said, tilting her head so that I had to look at her.

She laughed and invited me to her house. She told me that when we were alone, she didn't like to be called Mrs. Holly.

On the first visit to my teacher's house, I met her husband, Ed. He is handsome and nice; he shook my hand. He looked the way I imagined a husband should look, with his dark hair parted to the side.

"She's my best student," my teacher told him.

They stood there in their hallway together, he taller than she, and I imagined them making love.

When Ed went to work in his study, she told me he didn't like to fuck.

"Really?" I asked. My teacher was beautiful and I thought that everyone wanted beautiful women. If I were beautiful I was sure things would be different.

"So why don't you get a divorce?" I asked her. It was the first time I had been to her house.

"I don't know. I don't know why we even got married. It just seemed like a good idea at the time."

I watched her purse her lips and take the last drag of her cigarette.

"Ed will be done soon," she said, taking my cigarette from me and taking a drag, then putting it out in the ashtray.

I looked at the floor where beneath us, Ed was working.

"He seems nice," I said.

My teacher shook her head, "He doesn't like it dirty. We're not compatible."

My teacher told me about an ice sculptor she had met, a man who knew how to make love. She said they went into his freezer to cool themselves down, and she watched as he carved things: birds and bowls for restaurants and, for his art, a naked woman made of ice who dripped water from her crotch when she melted.

She wrote a poem about the ice sculptor. He wasn't as tall as she was, but he had thick arms that made her feel small.

We left her study and I followed her up the stairs to the bedroom. We lay on her big bed and looked at ourselves across the room in the mirror on the vanity.

"How old do you think I look?" she asked.

I did not know.

"Thirty," I said. "Twenty-eight?"

I was not good at telling people's ages.

"Really?" she said, pursing her lips. Her lips were shriveled in a strange way that reminded me of brains.

"I think so, yeah," I said.

She squinted and reached over to feel my face. I worried her hands felt each acne bump on my skin, but she smiled. She pushed my hair behind my ear.

"Wow," she said. "And you don't even own your face yet."

After class, the next week, my teacher pinched me under the table and wrote on her notebook, "I need to show you something. Stay after class."

When class was over we sat on the desk tops and closed the door.

My teacher opened her folder and took out a sheet of paper that was typed.

"Read this," she said.

I read the poem. It was short, about a neutered bulldog who was sad and thought no one would ever love him.

I looked up at my teacher who was looking at me, watching me read and smiling.

"I think I am missing something," I said.

"Really?" she asked. "I thought it was so obvious. Brian must feel inadequate. He must feel inadequate as a man."

"Brian Wojowsky wrote this?" I asked, looking again at the neat type writing, definitely from a real typewriter.

"Yeah," she said, taking the page back. "He gave it to me this morning during homeroom. Who would have thought? I mean, he never says anything, right? So talented . . . and how great that he can express himself this way. It's kind of sexy, even though he is admitting he might not be able to satisfy a woman."

She wasn't looking at me when she said this. She had her skirt bunched up at her knees and her feet on the chair. Someone could look in on us through the small rectangular window on the door.

"Yeah," I said, pretending I understood. It did not surprise me that I was missing something when she told me things. Sometimes it made me think everyone knew things that I didn't. It was as if all the things people whispered to one another, all the books I hadn't read, were the things I most needed to know.

"I wonder if he knows how good he is . . . " my teacher said, placing the page back in her folder, being careful not to crease it. "I should tell him," she said, nodding to herself.

My teacher calls me in the middle of the night. She whispers into the phone.

"I did it!" she says, "I saw it!"

"Saw what?" I say.

"The neutered bulldog!!" she says and laughs.

I am still half asleep, warm in my bed.

"Can we talk tomorrow?" I ask, even though I love her.

"Okay," she whispers, and hangs up the phone.

When I am at home, in my own house, I go upstairs and lock the door to the bathroom, where I lie on the thin bath carpet on the tile floor and try to think only about the things I can see. I look at the dust beneath the sink cabinet and the underside of the toilet bowl and up at the red heat lamps. I look out the top of the window at the black branches against the gray sky and feel sad and lonely.

Twice I have showered in the bathroom with all my clothes on, which felt strange and warm but in a good way until I turned the water off. Then I felt cold and disgusting, and my jeans stuck to me in a thick and heavy way. Usually I get in the shower without my clothes and sometimes I shave different parts of myself I hadn't before, like the backs of my hands and toes.

On the floor with the heat lamps on, I can only think about what I see until I think of something else. No matter what is in front of me, it seems, it never keeps all of my attention. I imagine Brian and my teacher, using up all the space on her bed. I imagine Brian so small next to her. Brian is just a boy in my class. She is big on her own bed. It occurs to me then, sadly, that this is what she wants.

It is Saturday so I drive to my teacher's for brunch. She mixes up a salad dressing from Balsamic vinegar and mustard and pours it over lettuce. She makes us chamomile tea.

My teacher is still wearing her nightgown. Her husband has been away for the week on a business trip. We sit alone at her sunny table and pick at our salads.

"So, I did it," she says.

"With Brian?" I say.

"Yes. And he has nothing to worry about," she says, shaking her head. "It won't be a problem for him. I think he'll be fine."

The First Hurt

My teacher doesn't know that I am still a virgin. When I tried to do it, once, with a boy with huge feet I met last summer, it hurt too much and he couldn't get it in. It did not feel good and I can't imagine it ever feeling any way but sore. I am told that once you start you will not want to stop, and I pretend to my teacher that I have started, with boys from the other school districts.

"Did you like it?" I ask.

"I think we are going to have to work on it," she says, swiping her highlighted hair from her face and letting the strap of her nightgown fall so that I can see the start of her nipple.

In math class, I watch Brian walk in. He does not look at me. He sits down across from me, his shaggy hair in his face, and begins to draw in his notebook. He has acne on his neck that it looks like he picked, and his shoelaces are untied. He does not look full, the way my teacher looked in the morning. His cheeks look like he is sucking on a straw.

I draw in my notebook. I try to picture how lesbians do it. I draw two vaginas squeezing each other with their lobes.

I ask to go to the bathroom and sit in the stall and smoke a cigarette. Brian is a loser, I think, and no one wants to date him in our class. Everyone loves my teacher. The boys who see me leave with her ask if I ever lick her pussy.

I put my head between my legs and get a head rush and try to picture Brian with his neutered dick. I picture my teacher on top, her freckled body astride small Brian. I picture them lying in the sheets afterward, looking at their reflections in the same mirror that my teacher and I did and laughing.

I go to my teacher's after school. She is sitting in the back-yard on one of her lawn chairs, her eyes closed and her face up to the sun.

"Come tan with me," she says, but I hate the sun. I pull a chair into the shade of her house.

Her garden is lined with bricks she put there herself. I have seen her some days, shovel in hand, trying to grow things. She wears a hat, like a woman with a garden in the movies.

"Where did you learn to garden?" I ask her.

Her past seems like something unreal, something that would never happen to someone like me. The way she talks about things seems so easy, like she slipped out of a bed some-where far away, already a woman with a husband and lovers, already with a past.

"My dad," she says. "He used to make us help him plant things."

She keeps her eyes closed and I stare at her. It is like she is asleep and I am spying, or she is dead and I am examining her, so close in a way that nobody would let anyone else look at them.

My teacher is wearing tight white jeans and a striped T-shirt. Her skin looks papery around her eyes and I can see the creamy cover-up she has on her face. There are white hairs on her cheeks, fine hairs that look soft. For a moment I won-der what would happen if I sat on her lap with my arm around her neck.

My father does not plant things. He makes me mow the lawn every weekend on a small tractor. He makes me wear headphones so that I do not lose my hearing from the loud noise the mower makes. He has a way I am supposed to mow: around and around in one big oval, then in smaller cir-cles when I get to the two big trees in the middle of the yard.

"I like to garden," she says. "It distracts me, you know?"

I do not know, but I nod. It is hard for me to get distracted that way. When I mow, all I can think of is the next circle, and then the next, and how when I am done I will be able to go inside and lie on the bathroom floor.

My teacher's eyes are still closed, and she does not see me nod. She opens one eye and smiles.

"Brian is coming over tonight," she says.

"Again?" I ask.

"Again," she says.

At home, in the bathroom, I lie on the floor and turn on the heat lamps and close my eyes. I think about my grandparents' old bathroom with a bidet that my mother once washed my underwear in when I peed my pants.

"What's it really for?" I had asked.

I had never tried the bidet then, and now that I am old enough, my grandparents have moved to a less fancy apartment.

I love the idea of being that clean after I go to the bathroom, hardly having to wipe. I love the idea of all that mess disappearing.

Someone knocks and my father's voice says, "What's going on?"

He must see the sliver of red glow beneath the door and worry.

"Nothing," I say.

In math class on Monday, Brian's shoelaces are untied. I wonder if he slept over at my teacher's or if he drove home late, listening to loud music down the long roads in the dark. I wonder if he is like me, and can only think of other things while he is in math class. I draw a woman with a long white skirt on my math test margin.

Mr. Hall, our math teacher, calls on Brian.

"And what did you get for number nineteen?" he asks. Mr. Hall wears wide ties with bright patterns on them. To get our attention, he says.

"Um," Brian says, shuffling through his papers.

"Dork," Alec Ryerson coughs into his armpit.

"Enough," Mr. Hall says, pointing at Alec.

"Brian?" he asks.

"Um. I didn't get that far," Brian says.

Brian's face is flushed. He is in the moment. He doesn't know what I know about him, that I know what he is thinking. That I know, I know. I did not even have to be there.

My teacher holds up a pair of plaid boxer shorts.

"They're his!" she says.

"Whose?" I ask.

"Brian's," she says, laughing.

Before I met my teacher, I thought only teenagers acted this way.

"Oh," I say.

Ed is on a business trip again and will be returning tomorrow. I wonder what she will tell him she did while he was away.

We sit on her couch, in front of the fireplace and drink tea. I look through a book on her coffee table. It is a book of photographs of trees.

"How are you going to see Brian when Ed gets back?" I ask.

"Oh, well," she says, sipping, "I have it all planned out. When Ed is at work Brian can come over and we can have our rendezvous in my study."

"Wow," I say. "Right above him?!"

"Yes," she says. "It turns me on."

I did not know that cheating was so easy. It is all a matter of time and space, it seems; when one person leaves a space, another person can fill it. When one person comes back, the other person leaves. Just like that.

If I squeezed over in my own bed there would be room for one more. There is also another bed in my room for sleepovers, but no one has slept there since eighth grade. Sometimes I switch beds for a few weeks and sleep in the empty bed. I wake up in the night and wonder where I am. The room is in the wrong place and I can see what every girl that ever slept there saw: my mother's old doll collection she passed down to me, the slant of the ceiling in stucco white, and my own empty bed, looking more cozy than it did before. After a few days, I crawl back into my own bed and wake up only to pee.

"Do you think my breasts are sagging?" my teacher asks me in the afternoon while she is changing into her bra. We are in her bedroom and I am sitting on the bed where she sleeps and does it with Brian.

It had not occurred to me that there was anything wrong with my teacher before. She had been a model. She is a poet, and after a new man makes love to her, she has a new poem in the morning.

"No, not at all," I say. I sit on my teacher's bed and watch her.

"You should try this on," she says, taking out one of her dresses from her closet. It is long and navy blue and goes out where her hips must have pushed it.

"I'll try it in the bathroom," I say, taking the silky dress off the hanger.

"Don't be silly," she says, catching me and pulling at the other end of the dress. "Try it on here."

I sit on the bed and take off my jeans and then my shirt, covering myself up quickly by putting the dress under my chin and then over my head. My teacher watches me and laughs.

"What are you doing?" she says. "You silly."

"Stand up," she says, and I do.

First my teacher pulls the dress all the way down. It is a bit big, but in the three-way mirror she turns me in front of, I can tell that it fits in the back.

"Look how nice you look," she says, and then she turns me around to face her. She looks into my eyes, and I laugh because for a moment I forget who I am. Then she lifts the dress above my head so that she can see everything but my face.

"Stop," I laugh. I try to pull the dress down with my hands but my teacher is tall and strong. She holds the material above my head so I can only see the outline of her through the fabric, and not what her mouth is doing.

I stop trying to bend over. I hold my hands above my head and surrender.

My teacher lets the dress fall back down.

"You're lovely," she says, pointing her finger at me.

"Shut up," I say. I wonder if she is teasing me. Or if she feels bad for me. I also wonder, enough to make me blush, if maybe she is telling me the truth.

In gym class we have to run the entire field. The gym teachers are all old men—stupid old men—who wear shorts that go down to their old men knees. They are tired old men who have been here too long. They don't even coach sports teams, they just watch us run in gym.

A bunch of kids go into the woods at the edge of the field and smoke pot. You can see through the trees when the gym teachers are calling them in and you can hear the whistles in the woods. These kids depend on the other kids, the nerds, to run around and around the field for the whole gym period. I usually go into the woods alone or else stand near the other kids and smoke cigarettes. When there is a big group, sometimes they don't notice me.

Today Brian is there, smoking a cigarette between two fingers like a girl, not like the other boys who hold it with their thumbs and look sexy. He looks stupid smoking; he has always been one of the runners. I wonder if he has only taken up smoking since he has taken up sex.

Alec Ryerson walks over to me and asks me for a light. He has blond hairs on his legs that are thick on his thighs. He has a joint.

"Hey," he says. "Hey, Sarah." He talks as if he is just remembering my name.

"Hey, Alec," I say.

I slump down and lean against a tree and light the joint for him. He leans over and looks down, and in the flame his eyelashes are dark and long.

Alec stands back and blows the pot smoke in my face.

"Brian says you eat Ms. Holly's pussy."

I look over at Brian who is looking out at the field.

"Shut the fuck up," I say to Alec.

"Brian," Alec calls over to him. "Didn't you say you saw Ms. Holly and Sarah in a sixty-nine?"

Brian looks at me and blushes. It seems to be the first time we have ever looked at each other. His eyes are small like mine.

"Yes," Brian says. He needs no coaxing from Alec. He is set on his lie, the way he insisted the neutered bulldog was about his "friend's brother" to my teacher before she got it out of him and then inside of her.

I look down at the ground where onion grass is growing up from the dirt.

"Jaime Dwyer says he saw you two at the movies once, too."

It was true my teacher and I had gone to the movies once, two towns away. We shared popcorn and a large diet soda and sat near the front, silently. We both cried—it was a sad movie about two people in love. During one scene, while the actors had sex, my teacher pinched my leg and twisted. I wanted to tell her I didn't like that, that I was sensitive.

I hadn't seen Jaime Dwyer there; I often missed other people when my teacher was around. When I was alone, I was always looking at people: kids in the halls who were trying to walk quickly without tripping, mothers who looked like their sons, picking them up in their vans after practice. With my teacher, I felt safe, like I had a blindfold on and she was leading me, her manicured hand pushing and pulling me.

"Whatever, asshole," I say.

I realize how much I hate Brian. I hate his smallness and his stupid poems. He is unremarkable and I notice everything.

"You stupid bitch," Brian says, out of nowhere. He flicks his cigarette like some tough guy and folds his arms across his chest.

Kay Simon, the class slut, pulls down her belly shirt so her breasts are flattened.

"Fight!" she says, walking over to where we are from where she was, wherever she was. "Fight!" she says.

Other kids start to come out from behind the trees like dwarfs who were hiding in *The Wizard of Oz*. Where were all these people before? They surround us, and for once it seems like Brian and I are popular.

I feel like I am in the middle of things, and I start to get a ringing in my ears. Brian and I are inside a group in the middle of the woods and in the center of my world. I can see his pores.

"Come on," Alec says, clapping his hands like he's trying to get a dog to come to him.

"Dyke," Brian whispers.

I get close to him like I will spit on him, but instead I say, "Neuter."

No one else can hear us, but Brian's face turns red.

The whistle blows. A gust of wind hits us. Brian and I can only see each other.

"Shit," Alec says, walking back to the field. Everyone else starts to follow. If we are not back by the second whistle we can get detention.

I watch as Brian walks with his head down, his hands in his pockets. I walk behind him, staring at the back of his greasy head. I walk in the footprints he makes in the misty field, noting that my footprints are bigger.

At home, my teacher calls.

"I want you to come over for dinner," she says, "and wear the dress."

The dress has been in my closet, hanging there as if it is waiting in the shape I hope to fill.

"Eight o'clock," my teacher says.

In the bathroom, after my shower, I lie on the floor and think of how I will tell her. I will move over to her side of the table and sit on her lap. I will stroke her hair off her face and put my finger to her wrinkled lips.

"Him or me," I will say. "Choose."

Then she will answer me with her hands or her tongue and I will find the words in her mouth, without her having to say them.

I smooth the dress on my hips outside my teacher's front door. I look down at the pouch of my stomach and suck it in. In my backpack are two packs of cigarettes and wine from my parents' cabinet.

I ring the doorbell and put one hand on my hip. I wonder where her husband is tonight.

When my teacher opens the door she is smiling. She is wearing a tight black minidress that hangs off the shoulder and her hair half up, half down. In the light, she looks like a club MTV dancer. I have never seen her so beautiful.

"Come in," she says, kissing me on the cheek. "You look fabulous."

"You do too," I say, putting down my backpack, and I walk into the living room. There, on the couch, sits Brian in a sweater and khaki pants, as if he thinks he is grown up. He holds a glass of red wine and motions it to me as if he is giving me a toast. He is smirking.

"You know Brian," my teacher says, "and I want you to meet Michael. He's the ice sculptor I was telling you about."

Michael is leaning on the fireplace mantle, looking at the photo book of trees. His blond hair is tied back in a ponytail, and I can see the veins in his big arms.

Michael shakes my hand and I start to feel a ringing in my ears.

"Good to meet you," he says, and I am surprised he does not have an accent.

I sit on the arm of the couch. I want to put my head between my legs but I don't. I feel like I am sweating through my dress.

"Want a cigarette?" Brian asks, opening his pack toward me. My teacher has gone into the kitchen and I wonder what everyone was talking about before I arrived.

I take one of Brian's cigarettes. He takes out a lighter and flips it open on his knee. He is stupid, and I think he must have practiced that move over and over the way I mouthed to my mirror, "Him or me?" I hate him.

"Here's some wine," my teacher says, pouring me a large glass.

Brian and I watch my teacher walk over to Michael. She puts her arm around his low waist and opens her legs. He puts his hand on her ass and moves it with his stubby fingers.

"Come up to my study," she says to him. "Let's pick out some music to dance to."

I have an urge to look at Brian and smirk, as if I am saying "we know what that means," but we have shared enough secrets, and we both know, without looking at each other, what we know.

I listen to my teacher's laughter while I trace the patterns in her rug with my foot. I hear the door shut, then a thump, then muted laughter, and then nothing. I wonder if Ed hears sounds like these and thinks she is bumping around her office, just writing poems.

"Oh God," Brian says, putting his head in his hands.

There is a place on the couch next to Brian, between us, that needs filling. I lean from the arm of the couch and slide my butt down. It feels easy moving this way, the red wine making me ache.

My hand touches Brian Wojowsky's back and I rub it in circles—first big and then smaller and smaller to the center of his back as if there was something there that needed kneading. In the center of Brian Wojowsky there must be something like that, but I do not say anything because we are not writing poetry. The poem, it seems, is where my fingers go, on the tiny bone I come back to each time the circle becomes a dot. It is not something we say in my teacher's house. It is not something we will write down.

Jewish Hair

Kenny D'Ambrosio and his father owned D'Ambrosio Meats. In the big front window of their store Ida could see them cut ham with their large hands and pack it into neat, white paper. They smiled with one side of their mouths, as if there was a secret joke between them and their customers. The secret could be about cold cuts, but it hinted at something else.

Ida took the long way home from her father's shoe store where she worked, so she could pass by and watch Kenny. From outside she could see behind the counter where father and son moved smoothly around each other. They never looked at one another, just seemed to know where each other's bodies would move: who needed the slicer, who needed to take out the chicken breast.

Ida wanted a reason to go inside. She could get a sandwich. But the men scared her, and she was afraid they would know that she had come for something else, and she would have: Ida's new stepmother, Janet, had left Kenny for Ida's father. Ida had never been interested in the butcher—had never gone there except when she was small with her mother, until Janet. Suddenly Kenny D'Ambrosio was connected to her: still a whiff of him somewhere on her stepmother.

When Ida was twenty she still wasn't married. She had a beautiful older sister who was married and lived upstate. Ida lived at home with her parents and walked to work with her father every day.

Ida wore the most fashionable shoes for women. She would stand up tall next to her father, a man everyone liked. He wore a hat with a maroon ring around it, and everybody knew him and called him "Mr. Boots." In a town that did not have many Jews, this was better than Mr. Feinstein. "Mr. Boots" was like a funny character, and Ida was his frail, sad daughter who had none of her father's charms.

Still, she made sure the shop was clean and the books were correct while her father flirted with the customers out front. After Ida finished high school and was able to work full-time, her mother stopped coming to the store. Before she died, she preferred the couch in the living room more than the chair at the shop.

All day long Ida was silent in the back of her father's shoe store—speaking only to her father when she had to. She did the books and then left after some time in the bathroom where she looked in the mirror and picked at her face.

In the back of the shoe store, Ida organized the receipts, did the books and the orders, and looked in the shoe mirror at her small ankles in her heeled, tie-up shoes. They were the most expensive shoes in the catalogs.

"I have perfect ankles," she thought.

Wouldn't she have been blessed if her whole body was as sleek and smooth as her ankles? Instead she had acne that her father took her to the doctor for. There, they flashed her face with radiation, a new technique that was supposed to help her skin. They turned off the lights and Ida squeezed her eyes shut while the doctor held the switch. She wished it hurt when the radiation was on, so that it would feel like something was happening. But it felt like nothing. And when the doctor turned the lights on again and she opened her eyes it was like she had been there for no reason. The doctor would always pat her back as she was leaving, reminding her to leave her face alone.

In the back of the store Ida lay on her stomach so that she could see her face in the shoe mirror. There she scratched the red spots on her cheeks. She pinched and squeezed until she became blotched. Then she went to the bathroom and splashed her face. She had pancake makeup that she scooped up to hide where she had picked. She sat on the toilet and waited until everything stopped bleeding.

Safe in the back, she continued with the books and wondered if it was like stashing chocolate, the way she hid what she did with her skin. She knew it was one of the reasons no one liked her in synagogue. If only, she thought, I could have perfect skin.

At twenty, the skin on Ida's belly was smooth and clear. At night she rubbed her feet together and thought about the men she knew. There was the rabbi who was still unmarried. There was something about him: the way he held the *yad* when reading from the Torah that made it look like the instrument was too fragile. It seemed far more fragile—it being metal—than it really was. But she also looked forward to seeing the Rabbi read. It felt good, in a way, to be disgusted by him. She did not want to be the Rabbi's wife.

Almost all of the other men were married to girls she had gone to high school with. She would see them with their children; if they had more than one they would dress their children alike.

In the pews she would imagine what she looked like to them. She understood: she would never want to marry herself.

Janet was the kind of woman you could see with anyone. She had two pairs of silk stockings, and the dresses she wore never let you forget her breasts. She had honey-colored hair and red lips that she painted into a small bow. She belted herself in at the waist so that you could see the way her hips went out in two bumps like a layer cake. Ever since Janet moved in, Ida ate in the den on the couch while she and her father ate in the kitchen. She refused to eat Janet's food (meatballs and thick spaghetti; chicken picata, which Ida didn't like the sound of). Ida ate oatmeal for dinner each night. She sprinkled cinnamon and sugar on her oats, then made her way to the couch.

At first her father protested, "Oh Ida. Why can't you eat with us? We miss you."

For a while he called from the kitchen, "Head-dyyyyyy," in a singsong voice, "my sweet."

Three months in and both her father and Janet ignored her. Ida would listen to their conversation (which consisted of their day the weather shoes co-workers nothing nothing nothing) and sometimes she yelled something in.

"That is a great dress on you," she heard her father say to his wife.

"It's ugly and cheap!" Ida yelled in.

In the beginning her father would yell back, "Ida, if you want to speak to us please come in here and sit down. Otherwise, stop it!"

Three months in and Ida had become a ghost.

"I heard that Kenny D'Ambrosio is thinking of buying another store," Ida yelled in one day after walking by the shop. It wasn't true—Ida had not heard anything. Ida liked to say "D'Ambrosio," even if Janet wasn't around.

Janet and her father ignored her—none of them had ever mentioned Kenny before—and Ida made smacking noises with her mouth while she ate the oatmeal. She thought of the teeth on Kenny—the two eyeeteeth that stuck out a bit and looked a little like a vampire, a little like he'd bite.

Tomorrow, Ida decided to get up her nerve and buy some meat. She could not decide what kind but then dreamed of capicole. She liked the word—it sounded tasty and had two ways of being pronounced. She had never tried it, and wanted a taste.

Ida wore her navy blue lace-ups with the heel and her matching navy blue wool skirt-suit even though it was warm out. She walked to the shop to order capicole.

She had looked in the dictionary. The way to say it was with the "e" at the end, it said. It was from a pig. She would throw it out before getting back to the house.

Ida took a breath and then opened the door to the shop. Above her a bell rang. Her hands in her gloves were sweaty and gross. They were gloves her mother used to make her wear to sleep so she wouldn't pick her skin in the night.

Kenny's father smoked a cigarette with his elbows on the steel counter.

"Hello, young lady," he said. "How are you doing on this lovely day?"

He smiled at her with his half smile.

Ida looked at all the meats. They looked clean, the way they were sliced down the middle; they were shaped in odd ways and she wondered what parts of what animal each one was.

"I'll have a half pound of capicole, please," Ida said.

"Capicole, coming right up," he said, pronouncing it like "soul," without the "eee."

Ida wondered if he said it on purpose to correct her, but then he smiled that way again, and Ida could see where his son came from. While he bent down in the case to get the meat, Ida stood on her tiptoes to see if Kenny was in the back.

"Would you like it thin?" Mr. D'Ambrosio asked. Ida didn't know.

"No. Thick, please. Very thick," she said.

"Okay, young lady," he said, slicing three thick pieces on the machine. He wrapped them up for her in white paper, folding it a certain way that looked special. He popped open a paper bag and handed her the package like it was a present.

Ida paid, and began to walk out the door.

"Have a nice day," Mr. D'Ambrosio said, and Ida smiled and looked behind her for Kenny once more.

Her money was wasted; there was no Kenny in sight. But she had enjoyed buying the food anyway. Perhaps Mr. D'Ambrosio thought she had a family who liked to eat capicole with green beans. Perhaps he thought that beneath her white gloves there was a heart-shaped ring with lots of karats. Perhaps he thought someone loved her, and she was buying food because she loved them too.

She looked back in the window at Mr. D'Ambrosio, who had his elbows back on the counter, smoking a cigarette. He looked like he wasn't thinking at all.

She began to walk away, then heard the sound of a bottle drop in the alley between the butcher's and the cleaner's. She looked down the long thin aisle where Kenny leaned against a wall, blowing smoke.

Ida stared at him. He picked up the bottle, and shook it in his mouth trying to get the last drops. It was alcohol, Ida smelled. Kenny turned and saw her.

"Hey," he said, and Ida started to run. She ran as fast as she could in her pencil skirt and shoes. She ran, hoping she wouldn't rip the stockings she had stolen from Janet's drawer. Ida ran, holding the ham in her hand, and dropped it on the street before her own. She ran until she got to her house, then went inside it to bolt the door and stand against it, panting, like she was being chased.

First Ida spritzed the perfume on herself, and then on the paper and in the envelope. The paper was pink. Ida didn't know why her sister Anita had given her this stationary last Hanukkah.

Ida had written a thank-you note for the stationery on the stationery that she had given her. Then she had put the rest of the paper in her desk drawer and had not used it since. After the paper was dry from the perfume, Ida wrote at the top of it:

March 4, 1946

Dearest Kenny,

I know that I am married now, but I still hold you in my heart. I made a huge mistake that only now I can see clearly. You are the most beautiful man I have ever met. I miss your voice, your smell, your arms and legs, your chest, your lips, etc. Kenny, you are a real man, even if you didn't go to war. Will you meet me next Friday evening outside Berdick's at six? I really need to speak with you.

Your love,

Janet

Ida wrote softly without digging into the paper the way she usually did. She sprayed the paper one more time, and then addressed it to Mr. Kenny D'Ambrosio. She put in her own return address without Janet's name, and put two stamps on it, just to make sure. Then she ran down to the mailbox at the end of the block in bare feet, before she lost her nerve.

Ida sat in the living room and picked her face. She took the small hallway mirror down with its metal circular frame that showed her small circular reflection, and stood it against the window frame in the living room. Then, opening Janet's ugly new curtains only a bit, she let the light in.

The sun was Ida's worst critic. It saw her even worse than she saw herself. It pointed out things she never would have noticed. It was scary, sometimes, to open the curtain. Things were always coming up a surprise.

Ida clapped when she squeezed her face too hard, waiting for the pain to go away. When she was younger, she made a friend from grade school take two handfuls of ice and slap either side of her face. All the tricks Ida knew to divert her one pain always caused another.

Ida always thought she wanted to be home alone more than she actually did. Without Janet to make fun of and her father to bother, there was no one to pick on but herself.

In the living room, her face turned red. She watched as the skin that had been fine before turned into a mess. She clapped her hands, then put the mirror back and washed her face. She looked up in the mirror and then went back to the couch.

Ida looked out the window and saw a man coming up the front porch.

She tried to look at his face but he was already in the doorway, ringing the bell, and the wood pillars on the porch blocked her view. She ran to the bathroom and quickly patted her cover-up on. The doorbell rang again.

"Coming," Ida yelled, running to the door in her new gray shoes. She no longer asked her father if she could order shoes for herself, she simply signed his name and bought herself what she wanted. Sometimes she opened her closet just to look at them.

Ida looked through the front door window. The man wore a butcher's bloody apron and a tight T-shirt. He waved at her through the door in a sarcastic way—swift and stiff. It was Kenny D'Ambrosio, and he had come to the wrong place.

Ida opened the door.

"Can I help you?" she said, the way she did when her father went to lunch and she had to wait on the customers.

Kenny's armpits were half yellow from old sweat and half gray from new.

"Where is Janet?" he asked, walking past Ida inside the house without asking.

"Janet!" he yelled up the stairs.

Kenny was sweating. His eyes were wide and blue. When he looked at Ida, he did not see her.

"She's at work," Ida said. "She works all day."

"Ha!" he said. "A fucking working girl!" He lit up a cigarette and held the pack out to Ida. She took one and he lit it for her, cupping the flame with his hand like there was wind.

Ida tried not to look at the scars on his arms. They had been covered with a tattoo on the inside of each wrist. One was a gun shooting out of an American flag and the other said "D'Ambrosio and Sons" with a roasted pig below in the outline of a heart inside another pig in the outline of a heart.

Ida sat down on the couch and put an ashtray out on the table from the drawer.

"Thanks," she said. Kenny D'Ambrosio was in her house and she was not scared. She knew what was next. She realized that she had no idea when Janet got out of work, and when she did not work at all.

She sat on the couch in the living room where the slats of sun made their smoke look delicate and complex.

Kenny sat down next to her and put his head in his hands, "I went yesterday to wait for her outside Berdick's. She sent me a note to meet her there, and then she didn't show."

He looked up and took a drag of his cigarette. Ida looked at the veins in his upper arms and wanted to touch them.

If I could be inside his head, Ida thought, I would know exactly what to do. I would pick up my ankles and comment on their perfectness, then kiss the bone on the inside, gently pulling up each perfect toe.

Kenny looked at Ida.

"What?" he asked. " I guess I shouldn't tell you any of this." He laughed, "What are you? Her fucking step-daughter?"

He laughed again and took out a flask that he drank from and then gave to Ida, who drank too. The taste was bad but the cigarette made it better.

"I guess so," she said. "Don't worry, though. I won't tell anyone you were here."

"Like I give a shit. She's the fucking whore. Trying to get me back while she's married to the old man. Fucking Jew!" he said, making a mean face that did not suit him. She had not known he could be mean.

He looked at Ida, whose face must have shown all these things.

"Sorry," he said, leaning back on the couch, "I'm fucking sorry," he said, looking at her, "I'm just mad. Really. I'm sad," he said, putting his hands over his eyes.

Ida did not know what to say.

"Do you forgive me?" he asked.

"I know it's not your fault."

Because it *was* Ida's fault, she forgave him for calling her father a "Fucking Jew." Because he took her hand then, and traced the veins, she forgave him. Because he put out his own cigarette, and then pulled the cigarette from her mouth and took a puff from it, she no longer cared. Because he put her cigarette out and unclipped her dark brown hair, she would let him call her father anything.

"Look at your thick hair," he said, putting it up to his nose and moving closer, "It smells so good."

Kenny smelled like meat and liquor. He smelled like a Thanksgiving dinner that forgot the cranberry sauce. Kenny's skin up close was as nice as it was far away. He leaned in to put his stubbly cheek to hers, then rocked her back and forth with him on the couch, petting the back of her head.

"Can I braid your hair?" he asked, and she turned around and let him as if she always let him do that. His fingers were so gentle, and she especially liked when he pulled the hairs up from her neck. She wondered how he had learned to braid. The whiskey had gotten to her, and when she turned for him it felt like she was sitting on a diner stool.

"You have Jewish hair," he said. "I like it."

He kissed the back of her neck and pulled her back so she was lying on top of him, her back to his chest. On her mother's couch, she let the butcher touch her from behind.

How did he know exactly how to touch her? She wondered. It seemed like a secret that he had found out. Suddenly, Ida felt a pain on her scalp.

"Ouch!" she said, and it happened again. Kenny was pulling her hair out, she realized, and it distracted her in a way she liked. It felt good after a while.

"I could make a rug with this," he said, pulling out more and more hair and placing it on her chest.

When he stopped, he touched her scalp, then dug his fingernails in. Ida wondered how crazy he really was. She always thought his craziness must be sad and confused. He did not seem like a man to her until she was lying in his lap.

"Turn around," he said, "and lift your skirt."

Ida did this. The light in the windows shone through on one part of his face.

Kenny sat on the edge of the couch, Ida in front of him with her hairy legs. She had never bothered to shave them. She had pictured and dreamed of herself in this position, but her legs were smooth and brown.

Kenny took one finger and peeled her big white panties aside from her crotch. The tip of his finger touched her, and he pulled her toward him.

"Now don't make any noise," he said, looking up at her for the first time, "or I will stop."

Then he put his tongue in between Ida's legs and Ida looked down, holding onto his shoulders. She gasped and he looked up.

"You new down here?" he asked her.

She did not know what to say. She felt old everywhere.

Then Kenny pushed aside his apron and she looked down to the bulge in his crotch.

"So you're the stepdaughter," he said, unbuckling his belt with one hand, keeping his finger steady inside her with the other.

She did not say a word, afraid he would stop. She would never speak again if he would keep his fingers inside her.

He pulled her down upon him and she gasped again.

"You're new," he said, smiling, and she rocked against him, holding on, the newest girl in the world.